The
Loud
Silence
of
FRANCINE GREEN

The Loud Silence of FRANCINE GREEN

by

KAREN CUSHMAN

CLARION BOOKS
NEW YORK

Clarion Books
a Houghton Mifflin Company imprint
215 Park Avenue South, New York, NY 10003
Copyright © 2006 by Karen Cushman

The text was set in 12-point Berkeley Book.
Book design by Michelle Gengaro-Kokmen.

www.houghtonmifflinbooks.com

Printed in the U.S.A.

Library of Congress Cataloging-in-Publication Data

Cushman, Karen.
The loud silence of Francine Green / by Karen Cushman.
p.   cm.
Summary: In 1949, thirteen-year-old Francine goes to Catholic school in
Los Angeles where she becomes best friends with a girl who questions
authority and is frequently punished by the nuns, causing Francine
to question her own values.
ISBN-13: 978-0-618-50455-8
ISBN-10: 0-618-50455-9
[1. Conformity—Fiction. 2. Catholic schools—Fiction. 3. Schools—Fiction.
4. Best friends—Fiction. 5. Friendship—Fiction. 6. Family life—California—
Fiction. 7. Los Angeles (Calif.)—20th century—Fiction. 8. United States—
Politics and government—1945–1953.] I. Title.
PZ7.C962Lou   2006
[Fic]—dc22   2005029774

QUM 10 9 8 7 6 5 4 3 2 1

For Nathan Adler, Lou Solomon, Philip Cushman,
and Trina Schart Hyman
for their courage and their example

Sooner or later one has to take sides
if one is to remain human.

—Graham Greene, *The Quiet American*

With thanks to Google for the research help,
libraries and librarians for being there,
and Arthur (Duffy) Lipski and Edward (Eddie) Cushman,
beloved little brothers, for the "Artie" parts

Contents

February 1950

March 1950

April 1950

May 1950

June 1950

The
Loud
Silence
of
FRANCINE GREEN

1

August 1949

Books and Beanies and Montgomery Clift

"Holy cow!" I said when Sophie Bowman told me she'd be joining me at All Saints School for Girls this year. "Why now, in the eighth grade?"

"Because I got thrown out of public school." Sophie and I were in the room I shared with my sister, Dolores. Dolores was on a date with her steady, Wally, so Sophie lay on Dolores's bed, her legs in the air, twirling the navy blue beanie from my school uniform on her foot. "It was either Catholic school or boarding school. No one else would have me. But Sister Basil thinks my soul can still be saved. From what I can tell, she's nuts about saving souls."

I sat up cross-legged on my bed. "Why?" I asked her.

"That's what she learned in nun school, I suppose."

"No," I said. "Why did you get kicked out of school?"

"Oh, that. For writing 'There is no free speech here' on the gym floor. In paint. Red paint."

She grinned at me as though that was the most wonderful

thing in the world. I didn't grin back. "Why on earth would you do that?"

"Because the principal banned radios in the lunchroom."

"Radios? You ruined the gym floor because of *radios?*"

She waved her beanied foot about. "Not just radios, dopey. It was a matter of free speech. Standing up for what you believe in. And fighting fascism."

Fascism? Wasn't that about Adolf Hitler? Did she mean Nazis kept her from playing the radio in the lunchroom?

"Harry says that he may agree with the sentiment, but the expression left a lot to be desired," she continued, stretching her long, summer-brown legs. I sighed and looked at my legs. They were pink and freckled like the rest of me.

"Who's Harry?" I asked her.

"My father. My mother went to Catholic school and he thinks she was nearly perfect, so off I go." I knew from Hettie Morris across the street, who knew Laurel Greenson, whose aunt was Mrs. O'Brien, who lived next door to the Bowmans, that Sophie's mother had died when she was born. "He wants me to be more like her and learn to express myself with patience, self-control, and moderation."

Sophie would be going to the right school. At All Saints we had patience, self-control, and moderation to spare and not a drop of free speech. I myself was so patient, moderate, and self-controlled that sometimes I felt invisible, and I liked it that way. Let others get noticed and into trouble. Let *Sophie* get into trouble. It seemed a sure bet that she would.

Sophie and I weren't friends or anything, although she

lived only a block down from me on Palm View Drive, in a pink stucco bungalow a lot like the one I lived in. We had nodded to each other over the years, and even played Red Light, Green Light together with the other neighborhood kids on hot summer nights. Now she had come over after dinner to learn more about All Saints, recognizing from my uniform that I was a student there. I couldn't imagine Sophie at All Saints, couldn't see her standing patiently in line in a blue sweater and plaid skirt—not the long-legged Sophie Bowman of the thick blond hair, outspoken opinions, and that lovely name, Sophie Bowman. Long mournful O sounds, so moody and romantic. Me? Francine Green, with Es like *eeek* and *screech* and *beanie*. Holy cow.

"I seriously hate beanies," Sophie said. "They make you look so drippy. Why do we have to wear uniforms like we're in jail?"

"It's not the same at all," I said. "Jails have much better uniforms. Black and white stripes, you know, are very fashionable this year."

"They are?"

"I was kidding, Sophie."

"Oh." Sophie wagged her beanied foot at me. "Maybe," she said, "we should find some way to express our individuality even if we're condemned to uniforms."

"You mean like wearing red shoes?" I asked.

"Yes!" she said, raising her arm with her fist clenched.

"And plastic jewelry and white blouses with cleavage?"

"It would be spectacular. Let's do it," she said.

I pretended interest in my bedspread. Bunny ballerinas.

3

Ye gods. "No, I couldn't," I said finally. "We'd get in trouble. And I have no red shoes or anything with cleavage. Or any cleavage."

We looked down at our chests and sighed.

My bedroom windows rattled, and I could hear palm fronds scraping along the street. Los Angeles and I were enduring a period of Santa Anas, the hot winds from the east that made tempers and temperatures rise and your skin itch.

I got up to open the window in hopes of some cooler night air. "Look," I said, "searchlights. There's a movie premiere somewhere."

Sophie got up and stood next to me at the window.

"Don't you love living so near Hollywood?" I asked her. "I mean, movie stars are right there, at the bottom of that light. Gary Cooper, maybe. Or Clark Gable. Or Montgomery Clift. Imagine, right there. Montgomery Clift."

"Montgummy who?" Sophie asked.

"Are you kidding me? Montgomery *Clift*. He's only the dreamiest dreamboat in the whole world, with the saddest brown eyes." I sighed and looked again at the searchlight connecting me to Montgomery Clift. "He's my absolute favorite. Who's yours?"

"I don't know much about movie stars," Sophie said.

"But Hettie Morris said your father writes for the movies."

"He writes them, he doesn't go see them. He wants us to read books to improve our minds. Good books. Serious books. Boring books. Oh nausea."

"He sounds like Sister Basil. She's always making us read

holy, dull-as-dishwater books." I thought for a minute. "Don't you get tired of improving your mind?" I asked her. "I would."

"Sure, sometimes. But you can't improve the world until you improve your mind, I always say." She smiled. "Actually, I don't always say that. I just made it up. Pretty good, don't you think?"

I nodded. "But jeepers, you could take a day off now and then. Just read a novel or a comic book or something."

"Okay, like what?"

"Well," I said to her, "you have come to the right place. There is nothing here that will improve your mind." I walked over to my dresser and examined the clutter on top. Dolores had a pink-skirted dressing table in our room, so there was no space for me to have a desk. I thought that said something about what was important in the Green household. "Let's see. Archie comic? Donald Duck? *Stories from the Bible?*" The only other book I owned was *Stuart Little*, which my aunt Martha and uncle George had sent me for Christmas last year. I held it up. "How about this," I asked her, "about a family with a son who's a mouse?"

Sophie frowned.

"Okay, you're a little old for that." I tossed her a copy of *Modern Screen* magazine. "Take this. It has a story about Montgomery Clift. You can borrow him until you get a favorite of your own."

"Don't you think movie stars and fan magazines are a bit frivolous and juvenile?" She took the magazine anyway and hopped back to Dolores's bed. The magazine fell right open to a picture of Monty. Sophie took out the dried banana peel I had used as a place marker and studied the photo. "Jeepers," she said, "he *is* good-looking. Kind of shy and haunted, like he's been persecuted and misunderstood."

The telephone in the hall rang. I could hear my little brother, Artie, answer it, "Duffy's Tavern, Archie the Manager speaking," just like the guy on the radio show. Artie liked *Duffy's Tavern*. He said he would own a tavern just like Duffy's when he grew up if he wasn't going to be a cowboy. Artie says things like that. He's five.

"Is it for me?" I called to him.

"It's for Dolores, like it always is," he said, sticking his head in. His yellow cowlick was standing straight up from the back of his head, and his glasses hung from the very tip of his nose. "Where is she?"

"Out," I told him, "like she always is." Artie left. I flopped back onto my bed. "It's so depressing being the sister of Miss Popularity. I'm surprised I don't have a complex."

"Don't you get along with her?"

"Are you kidding? Dolores hates me. If she could, I think she'd return me, like underwear that doesn't fit."

Sophie looked puzzled. "I don't think you can return under—"

"Never mind. It was just a joke. I meant that she'd like to get rid of me. I wish she was someone else's sister."

"Still, she's your family. I think you'd be awfully lonely being an only child."

"Are *you?*" I asked her.

"No," she said, "but I think *you* would be."

I leaped up and began jumping furiously on my bed. "We're acrobats on the trampoline," I shouted as I bounced onto Dolores's bed, "and we're gorgeous and popular and everybody loves us and we're never lonely and—"

Dolores blew in like the Santa Ana wind. "Stop it!" she shouted. I stopped. "Get off my bed. And get her off!"

I jumped down. "This is Sophie. She's a friend of mine from school. Or she will be when—"

"I don't care. Get her off my bed. And get out of here. Both of you."

"It's my room too."

"Who cares?"

Sophie got off the bed. Dolores flopped onto it and kicked her shoes across the room.

Sophie walked regally to the door, stopped, and looked back over her shoulder. "Gee, Francine," she said, "she's not *nearly* as pretty as you said."

Dolores stuck her tongue out, and Sophie stuck hers right back.

"Wow, Sophie," I said once we were safely out the door. "That was great." We slapped hands.

In the hall we bumped into Artie and his stuffed bear, Chester. Rice Krispies spilled from Artie's pockets and snap-krackle-popped as we walked over them. Sophie looked at me quizzically. "He carries them in his pockets in case of sudden starvation," I told her.

"Little kids are such a mess," she said, scraping Rice Krispies off her shoe. "I can't stand them."

"Artie's okay. He's sweet. Unlike Dolores."

Sophie shrugged and left.

I pushed Artie's glasses back up his nose. "Almost time for *Dragnet*," I said, taking his hand.

"Dun da dun dun," he sang, like the *Dragnet* theme song. *Dragnet* was one radio show Artie and I wouldn't miss for anything. We sat on the floor in the living room, our backs against the big radio. When we heard Jack Webb say, "This is the city. Los Angeles, California," we whooped and clapped. Los Angeles was *our* city.

After that day, Sophie and I were friends. Good friends. On the way to being best friends. It's funny how that happens, so suddenly, first just neighbors and then best friends.

2

September 1949

Sophie and the Trash Can

"Sophie," I said to her as we waited for the bus after school, "I never knew anyone before who got in trouble her first day. I told you to lay low and not talk back to Sister."

"I just wanted to ask some questions. I do have freedom of speech, you know." Sophie adjusted the pleats in her plaid skirt. She looked gorgeous in her uniform, like a teen model showing off the latest in Catholic-school fashions.

"You were supposed to ask *me* when you want to know something," I said. "Nuns have pretty strict ideas about asking questions and talking back."

Sophie said nothing, but the muscles in her jaw tensed. I guessed she was remembering this morning.

We had been circling adverbs and adjectives in our workbooks when Sister Basil clapped sharply. Sister Basil the Great was the school principal as well as the teacher of our eighth-grade class. She was not too old and very sweet looking with her green eyes, red cheeks, and snub, freckled nose.

I think it's wrong when people look like something they're not. Take nuns, for example. Friendly nuns should be plump and soft, like Sister Saint Elmo. Pious nuns, like Sister Anacletus-and-Marcellinus, should be skinny, quiet, and timid. And mean, nasty nuns like Sister Basil should look like Bela Lugosi in *Dracula*, not like a merry colleen on a Saint Patrick's Day card.

"Put away your workbooks, girls," Sister Basil had said. "It's time for morning prayers." I knew what that meant: prayers for the conversion of Russia. Sister was passionate about the conversion of Russia. Why, we'd said so many prayers for the conversion of Russia in this school since Sister became principal that I was surprised the Russians weren't all saints by now and praying for *us*.

We closed our books and knelt down in the aisles next to our desks. After a quick Our Father and Hail Mary, Sister Basil said, "Our Lady, holy Mother of God, we humbly beseech you to intercede for us with your divine Son that we may be with Him forever in Paradise. Ask Him to halt the Red Tide pouring out from Russia and lead the Godless communists to the True Church, for only then will there be salvation for the Russian people and true peace for us all. And, if it be His will, may we be victorious over Saints Peter and Paul today on the volleyball court."

I knew Saints Peter and Paul was a school, like All Saints, but still I imagined two old bearded saints in robes playing volleyball. I gurgled in my throat at the picture but didn't dare laugh out loud. Sister Basil would tie my tongue to the flagpole or something.

Sophie gave a muffled snort. It was not muffled enough.

Sister Basil rose from the ground like a column of smoke. "Stand up," she commanded. We stood.

"Not *all* of you," Sister said, grabbing her pointer and smacking it on the floor. "Just Miss Bowman." The rest of us knelt down again. I leaned back against my heels. This could take a while.

"You have a comment, Miss Bowman?"

"It just seemed silly, Sister, praying to win a ball game. Does God really care who wins?"

"That will do, Sophie."

"And what if students at Saints Peter and Paul School pray too? What will God do?"

"That's *enough*, Sophie."

"And why we are praying to win a volleyball game anyway when there are real problems in the world?"

Sister Basil banged her pointer on the blackboard. "Blessed Harvey, patron saint of croaking frogs, save me from this child!"

"And—"

Sister lunged at Sophie, grabbed her by her hair, and pulled her to the front of the classroom. "Enough! Enough of your interruptions, your blasphemy, and your impertinence! Here," she said, pointing to the wastebasket in the corner, "stand here where everyone can see you. And think about your sins." Sophie stood next to the wastebasket, but Sister grabbed her hair again. "No, Miss Bowman, *in* the basket. And don't slouch." Her green eyes flashed like traffic lights.

Sophie's eyes met mine. She looked puzzled and embarrassed. Every All Saints girl knew that this was the fate of those Sister hated, those who failed arithmetic quizzes, or forgot to raise their hands before answering, or seemed likely to lead the rest of us straight to Hell. I had told Sophie. Didn't she believe me? I looked down at my desk as Sophie stepped into the wastebasket.

"Now, girls," Sister Basil said, "let us finish our prayers." She was smiling.

Parents often remarked on Sister's sweet smile, but I knew what that smile meant. Sister smiled when she made Susan Murphy stay in at recess for laughing inappropriately, when she sent Gert Miller home with a note about her grades, or when she threatened noisy students with the wastebasket. When Sister smiled, the backs of my legs prickled with fear.

So we prayed, with Sister smiling and Sophie in the wastebasket. Then we did geography. I finished my work-sheet early and let my eyes wander over the classroom: the crucifix in the center of the front wall, flanked by pictures of Saint Barbara being hit with a hammer and Saint Agnes, patron saint of virgins and Girl Scouts, with a bleeding lamb in her lap; the wooden desks in neat rows (close enough to squeeze in as many as possible but not so close that anyone could cheat, which Sister assumed all students would do if they could); the mission box on Sister's desk, where we collected pennies and nickels to send to the pagan babies in Africa; the pull-down map of the world with the Soviet Union and parts of Germany colored red; the flag in one corner of the room and the statue of the Virgin in the other; the green paper window shades pulled exactly halfway down; the pencil sharpener fastened by the door—anything to keep my eyes from landing on Sophie, who was still standing in the wastebasket, her back as straight as a soda straw.

Finally the bell rang for recess and we all filed out, crossing in front of Sophie, who stood silent and unmoving. She did not look away or down but right into each of our faces as we walked past her.

It looked like Sophie was going to be Sister Basil's Victim of the Trash Can for 1949–50. Every year she picked a new favorite, or unfavorite, I should say, to torment. Last year it had been Betty Bailey, with her hair bleached lemonade yellow, her chest too big and skirt too short. Betty left school in January. Margie McGonigle said Betty was pregnant and went to a home for unwed mothers in Arizona. It was hard to believe, even of Betty Bailey, but if true, I guess it was a small price to pay for getting away from Sister Basil.

"Is she crazy, making me stand in a trash can?" Sophie asked once we were settled in the bus. "There are probably cooties and germs in there."

"That's the way Sister punishes girls who talk back or do other things she doesn't like. I told you. Sister likes to pick on people. She's plain mean. Just be quiet and do what you're supposed to, and it won't happen anymore."

"Oh, I don't really care. Other teachers have done worse. But it just isn't right. I wanted to ask some questions," Sophie said again, "and I was punished for the sin of intellectual curiosity."

"That's the way it is in Catholic school," I told her. "Why,

13

once last year, Susan Murphy asked Sister Immaculata if nuns wore black underwear under their black habits, and she had to spend a whole week in the second grade. Nuns don't much like questions."

Sophie rubbed her forehead slowly, disarranging her bangs, and tucked her hair behind her ears. "Is it so wrong to want to know things? Should I be punished for that? What about free speech, as guaranteed in the First Amendment to the Constitution?"

"In this school they care more about sin than free speech," I told her.

"Well, it's not right," said Sophie. "It's fascism, that's what it is."

"Wait, Sophie," I said. "You keep saying 'fascism' like it's something I'm supposed to know about. I know it's a bad thing and has something to do with Hitler and Nazis, but I don't think that's what you mean."

"Fascism? Well, it means having a dictator, using censorship and violence to stifle free speech and people's rights, making everyone conform and obey in silence." She got louder and louder. "Fascism is what you have in this school, and it's not right!"

While I brushed my teeth that night, I thought about Sister Basil and the way she had treated Sophie. I wished I could tell Sister how wrong it was, although I couldn't imagine speaking up to her. I dreaded the idea of standing in the wastebasket, but what I really feared was her smile. Now, if she were a strict but sweet and lovable nun like Ingrid Bergman, who starred as Sister Benedict in the movie *The Bells of St. Mary's* . . .

"Sister Basil the Great," I said to the mirror—Sister liked it when we called her by the full name, Basil the Great, to distinguish it from all the other Basils who were not so great, I supposed. I myself thought of her as Sister Basil the Not So Great. Or Sister Basil the Rotten. "Sister Basil the Great," I said again, "I wish to speak with you about Sophie Bowman. I don't think you should have been so mean to her and made her stand in the wastebasket on her first day of school."

"I must keep order in my classroom," I said, being Sister with a mouthful of foaming toothpaste, "and Sophie was being disruptive."

FRANCINE: She is merely curious and, being from public school, doesn't know about raising her hand, obeying without question, and suffering in silence. We must give her a chance.

SISTER: You are right, Francine. Jesus spoke of charity and understanding, and I have practiced neither.

FRANCINE: Actually, I don't think anyone should stand in the wastebasket. It hurts their feelings.

SISTER: Forgive me, Francine.

FRANCINE: I forgive you, Sister. Upon further thought, perhaps you could make the Perfect and Admirable Mary Agnes Malone, that stuck-up snitch, stand in the trash can, but no one else.

The end. That's the way it would be in the movies. I took a bow and spit into the sink.

3

Flowered Skirts and Paper-Doll Saints

"Look, Francine," Susan Murphy said, pointing to the hem of her skirt. "Isn't it delicious?"

I examined the skirt closely. There, drawn in black ink in the white parts of the blue, green, and white plaid, were flowers—roses and daisies, tulips and lilies. "Ye gods, Susan," I said to her, "you're ruining your uniform. Sister will blow a gasket."

"Who cares?" she said. "This is the last year I have to wear this crummy skirt. I want to see how long it takes Sister to notice."

"Ten seconds, I'd guess," I told her.

I was wrong. Sister didn't notice all that day. The next day, when Sophie and I arrived at school, there were Susan, Gert Miller, Margie McGonigle, and even the timid Florence Bush under the big palm tree near the front door, inking flowers on their skirts.

"Wow!" said Sophie. "What a swell idea." She pulled a

pen from her book bag, flopped down next to Margie, and began to draw. "Come on, Francine. I have extra pens, if you need one."

I shook my head.

"She won't do it," Gert said, pointing at me with her pen. "She never does anything fun."

It was true. I never did. Not if it would get me in trouble. "All great artists need an audience," I told Sophie. "You draw and I'll be your audience."

The bell rang for class. "Let's show our skirts to Sister," Sophie said. "It could be a protest against uniforms."

"Not me," said Margie, "and don't you dare either. You'll get us all in trouble."

"So what?" asked Sophie.

"You can be as weird as you want, Sophie Bowman, and get in all the trouble you want," said Gert, "but leave us out of it."

"Cowards," said Sophie.

"Oddball," Margie muttered as they turned to go inside.

Sophie looked at me. "I don't suppose you will either," she said.

I shook my head.

"At least do one flower." She held her pen out to me. "Just one. I'll go in if you'll draw one flower."

I took the pen and drew a tiny daisy, on the inside hem of my skirt where it couldn't be seen. "There. One flower. Now let's go."

We caught up with the rest of the girls in the hallway. I

examined their skirts. They were definitely more lively with little black flowers amidst the plaid.

I envied those girls. My own little hidden flower was a poor effort. I wished I was able to draw flowers on my skirt or paint faces on my knees or smoke behind the building after school like some of the others, but I never dared. I'd never been in trouble at school and had a knot in my stomach at the very thought.

By the beginning of fourth grade, I knew I would never be part of the lively crowd, the ones who had fun. I was too busy keeping out of trouble. So I decided to make friends with Mary Agnes Malone. She was pious and well-behaved, as boring as white rice, but she and her friends never got in trouble and were certain to go to Heaven, said the nuns. Besides, I was lonely.

I started by saying the rosary with Mary Agnes and her friends every day at lunchtime, even though it meant putting down my library book and leaving the Bobbsey twins or Rufus Moffat in some scrape I couldn't imagine how they could get out of.

One Sunday afternoon I was invited to Mary Agnes's big house off Wilshire Boulevard. Weslia Babchuk, Mary Catherine Parker, and Lois LaCroix were there too. We prayed, talked about homework, and had milk and vanilla wafers.

"Next week bring your paper dolls," Mary Agnes said as I was leaving. I skipped home. I loved paper dolls. I could create a whole world just the way I wanted it, with a brave, outspoken, colorful, popular Francine. I was in charge, my dolls did whatever I told them to, and none of us got in trouble.

My paper dolls were movie stars. Doris Day, Mona Freeman, and Betty Grable each lived with her clothes in her own separate See's candy box, the one-pound size. They had not only the dresses they came with but also special outfits I drew and colored, and socks, bathing suits, and pajamas I cut out of the Sears catalog.

I grinned as I packed up Doris, Mona, and Betty that next Sunday. We were about to meet new people and have glorious adventures.

After Mary Agnes led us in a Hail Mary, we all pulled out our paper dolls. "Doris Day? We don't play movie stars," Mary Agnes said. She handed me something that looked like a tiny black paper bathrobe. "Have her wear this. You can play she is Saint Rose of Lima." So Doris became the holy Saint Rose, and poor Mona Freeman had to be Saint Lucy and pluck out her own eyeballs.

I lasted only four Sundays before I began to make excuses not to go to Mary Agnes's. Paper dolls weren't nearly as much fun when they had to be made to pray and fast and act like saints. The last straw was when Betty Grable was torn apart by lions in a glorious martyrdom. I picked up the pieces and took poor Betty home, where she was miraculously healed through prayer and Scotch tape. The paper dolls and I stayed home on Sunday afternoons after that.

In the fifth grade Mary Agnes gave her paper dolls away for Lent, and she began putting all her spending money in the mission box for the pagan babies in deepest Africa. Sister

Saint Elmo said Mary Agnes's actions were perfect and admirable. I told Betty and Doris and Mona all about it as I colored new ball gowns for them.

All that remembering made me thirsty as I rode the bus home after school. I got off on Pico Boulevard and went into Petrov's Groceries and Fresh Meats. The store was dark and smelled of dust and overripe bananas. I pulled a bottle of Coke from the icy water of the cooler.

"You will rot your teeth, you young people and your Cokes," Mrs. Petrov said, shaking her finger at me from behind the counter.

"Don't worry, Mrs. Petrov, I brush." I took a big gulp of the Coke, so cool and bubbly and sweet going down. "How's Mr. Petrov today?" Mr. Petrov had a bad heart. He sat in the back of the store and listened to baseball on the radio while little Mrs. Petrov did all the work. Sometimes he'd take his chair out front and sit in the sunshine, eyes closed, eating cherry Popsicles and singing slow, sad songs in Russian.

As Mrs. Petrov took my nickel, she shook her head. "He is not well, not well at all."

I had another nickel in my pocket. I'd planned to put it in the mission box at school, but apparently I wasn't as perfect and admirable as some people, for I pulled it from my pocket and gave it to Mrs. Petrov. "I'll take a cherry Popsicle, too," I said.

I took the Popsicle outside. "Here, Mr. P," I said as I passed his chair. "This is for you from the missionaries in Africa."

He opened his eyes and looked puzzled as I handed him the Popsicle. But he nodded as he took it from me.

4

Lamb Chops à la Shoe Leather
and Dinner at the Greens'

The next week Sophie invited me over for dinner. "My father is cooking," she said. "Lamb chops à la shoe leather and lima beans. And martinis, but we don't get any of those."

"My father calls them martoonies," I told her.

"Oh nausea," she said.

Mr. Bowman shook my hand solemnly when I got there. He was very tall and thin, with long fingers like a piano player. His glasses, like Artie's, sat on the end of his nose. Tying an apron over his shirt and tie, he sang while he fried the lamb chops.

"*The Marriage of Figaro,*" Sophie whispered. "Opera."

"Sounds more like *The Murder of Figaro,*" I whispered back. She grinned and nodded as we sat down at the table.

"I had to stay after school today," Sophie said before she even took one bite. Jeepers, I thought, was she asking for trouble, dumping it on him right away like that? I tried to look invisible as I chewed.

Her father just sighed and finished his martini. "Why this time?"

"I merely asked Sister Basil a question. Just one question and she blew a gasket."

Mr. Bowman chewed slowly for a long time, probably trying to get the shoe leather soft enough to swallow. "And the question was?"

"She was talking about Maria somebody who should be a saint because she was martyred for refusing to act in what Sister called 'an unholy manner' with the farm boy. I asked her what she meant by unholy. Talking back? Missing Mass? Necking and petting? How unholy? She said never mind the details. We should just pray to be like the Blessed Maria. 'You mean get *murdered*?' I asked. She called me blasphemous and, zowie, after school. She said my curiosity and outspokenness were vicious habits."

"Sophie, my darling, you do not have to ask every question that occurs to you. Or say everything you think. Remember, patience, moderation, and self-control."

Was that all Mr. Bowman was going to say? Was Sophie in the clear? If I did something like that, I would be sent to my room until the year 2000!

"What about you, Francine?" Mr. Bowman was asking.

I gulped down a mouthful of lima beans. "Me? I didn't do anything."

"Of course not. I was merely asking about your day. I take it you were released at the normal time?"

I nodded. "It was fine. We collected almost a dollar for the pagan babies and did word problems in arithmetic," I said. "Sophie is real good at word problems."

"It must be her affinity for words of all kinds," Mr. Bowman said. "Especially 'fightin' words.'"

"Wonder where I get it," Sophie said, and took a big gulp of her milk.

After dinner Mr. Bowman picked up his newspaper while Sophie and I cleared the table. "I see in the *Times* that the Council of the North Atlantic Treaty Organization is meeting in New York," he said. "Nations working together for peace and protection. What do you girls think? Will that make us safer?"

I stood still with my stack of plates, speechless at the very thought of a grownup asking my opinion about anything more than "chocolate or vanilla?" but Sophie said, "It's a start, I guess, but I think it's all useless unless they ban the bomb."

"But Sophie, I'd say it's fear of Russia and communist nations in general that prompted the creation of NATO. I doubt they'll ban the very weapons they see as protecting us from Soviet aggression."

"Probably not," she said, pausing with her hands full of knives and forks, "but I'd feel a lot safer if people were out there fighting with sticks instead of bombs."

"You do have a point, my darling," Mr. Bowman said, laughing. "What do you have to say about international peace and security, Francine?"

Me? What? Did Mr. Bowman really care what I thought?

He had the same martini-and-cigarette smell my father had but otherwise was nothing like my father or indeed any other grownup I knew. Finally I managed to squeak out, "I think it would be a good idea."

Mr. Bowman nodded. "Indeed, Francine, indeed."

I walked home puzzled, as if I'd been in France or Poland or someplace where they spoke another language. I mean, dinner at my house last night went like this:

Scene: It's an ordinary family home. To the left is the dining room, elegant in brown wallpaper with gold roses and green leaves. The dining-room table is polished and gleaming. No one is eating there. No one ever eats there. At right is the kitchen—tan linoleum floor, tan cabinets, white curtains with a border of red cherries. Gathered around the kitchen table are a woman of middle years in gold-wire glasses, her fine brown hair in a sausage roll (Mother); her husband (Father) in blue tie and bifocals; a skinny boy of five in horn-rimmed glasses much too big for his little face (Artie); and his beautiful, sweet older sister (me, Francine, of course—20/20 vision). There is an empty chair because the oldest girl, a vicious hag of sixteen named Dolores, who needs glasses but pretends she doesn't, is being sent away from the table for wearing her hair rolled up in pin curls at dinner.

DOLORES *(stomping from the room)*: You don't want my hair to be curly. You want me to be ugly. You want me to have stringy hair and never get married and stay here with you the rest of my life! I'd rather die.

FATHER: Pass the meat.

MOTHER *(passing something vaguely meat-like to her husband)*: Arthur drew a picture of a duck in school today, didn't you, Arthur?

ARTIE *(his mouth full)*: Hmmumm.

MOTHER: I think Arthur is very artistic. Maybe he should be taking art lessons.

FATHER: How about another martooni, Lorraine?

FRANCINE *(silently)*: Oh nausea.

MOTHER *(returning to the table with Father's martini)*: How was school today, Francine?

FRANCINE: Fine.

MOTHER: And how is Sophie liking it?

FRANCINE: Fine, I guess.

MOTHER: Why "I guess"?

FRANCINE: I don't know. I assume she likes it okay. She's used to getting in trouble at school.

FATHER: Trouble? What kind of trouble? I don't want you getting involved with troublemakers.

FRANCINE: She kind of talked back to Sister Basil.

FATHER *(putting his martini down so hard it sloshes on the table)*: "Kind of"? There is no "kind of" talking back. I don't want to hear about you doing that. You are not there to bother the holy sisters.

FRANCINE: I know. But she only—

MOTHER: That's enough, Francine.

FRANCINE: I just—

FATHER: Lower your voice, Francine.

FRANCINE: I—

FATHER: Francine, be quiet!

ARTIE: Pass the meat.

Fade out

I tried to imagine my father asking what I thought about world events:

FATHER *(takes a deep puff of his cigarette. The smoke circles his head as he speaks)*: Francine, my dear, what do you think about godless communists and their evil desires to take over the world? How best can we stop them?

FRANCINE: Why, Father, I'm glad you asked. I am of the opinion that—

FATHER: And what do you make of current efforts to promote peace in the world?

FRANCINE: Well, Father, I—

FATHER: Pass the meat.

My imagination just wasn't up to the task. Holy cow.

5

October 1949

The Post Office, the Piggly Wiggly, and the Bomb

"I want to go too," Artie said.

"No."

"Pleeeease?"

"Take him with you," my mother said, handing me three dollars for stamps. "You know how he loves the post office."

"The post office is a silly place to love."

"Never mind. Just take him. And if I hear you were unkind or let him get lost, there'll be trouble."

Obviously I had no choice. Sophie should have painted "There is no free speech in this place" on our living-room floor. "Get a jacket," I said to Artie. "And wash—"

He jumped up. "I know. Wash my hands. Get rid of the Germans," he said.

"Germs, Artie."

"Germans," he repeated.

Artie and I left hand in hand for the post office. He had put on last year's Easter suit: short brown pants and jacket, long brown socks, and a matching beanie. It was too small for him, but our mother made him wear it anyway because it cost $3.97 and wasn't worn out yet.

"It's a long walk," I told him. "Don't say I didn't warn you." He dropped my hand and raced ahead of me up the street.

Palm View Drive ended at the ivy-covered stucco wall of the Twentieth Century Fox studio, where movies got made and dreams came true. I walked past the studio every chance I got, hoping sometime to glimpse a movie star or, even better, the head of the studio, and he would discover me and I, Francine Green, would myself be a movie star. I knew I would love being an actress. I could pretend to be someone else entirely, and not me, tongue-tied and empty-headed, at all. I had never seen a movie star or the head of the studio in all the years we'd lived on Palm View Drive, but it could still happen. I kissed my fingers and touched the wall for luck.

Artie and I turned onto Pico, where he let me catch up to him. "Why aren't we taking the bus?" he asked.

"Because I don't have nickels to throw away. Now stay close."

After three more blocks Artie began to drag his feet. After five blocks he began to whine, "Fran-*seeeeen,* don't go so fast." We slowed down.

Seven blocks into the walk, he stopped dead and said, "I don't want to go to the post office anymore. It's too far."

"Well, I'm not walking you all the way back home and then starting over again. It's only a little ways yet. Come on." I reached for his hand.

28

"No." He sat right down on the sidewalk.

"I'll tell you a story."

He looked up at me. "About a cowboy?"

"Yes, if you want."

He got up. I brushed the dirt off his pants and took his hand, and we started to walk again. "So, once upon a time, there was a beautiful princess who—"

"About a *cowboy*, Fran-*seeeeen*."

"There was a beautiful princess," I repeated, "who loved a cowboy."

"No, no love stuff."

"Well, he'd have to love his horse."

"That's okay. Just no love stuff with princesses or girls."

"But that's how this story goes," I said. "You can't just change a story."

"Then tell another story. One about cowboys and horses and no girls."

"Never mind. We're here." And we were.

The post office was crowded. I stood in line, looking at the criminals on the wanted posters on the wall—mostly angry-faced men with mean eyes who needed shaves. I examined the photos closely, but I didn't recognize anyone. Perhaps they were not pursuing their lives of crime in Los Angeles. Artie, meanwhile, helped himself to a handful of change-of-address cards, peeked into the mailboxes, and got in everyone's way. The Rice Krispies in his pockets dribbled out onto the floor and snap-krackle-popped as people stepped on them.

Finally the clerk took my money, gave me a roll of

three-cent stamps, and stamped "First Class" on Artie's hand.

Before heading home, we walked around a bit. Artie stared at his stamped hand while I admired the fall dresses in the shop windows. The new fashions were darkly romantic: wools and cotton plaids, with full skirts, wide collars and capes, and peplums that nipped the waist and flared out over the hips. "Look at that blue and green one, Artie. Isn't it just drooly? Artie? *Artie?*"

He was gone. In only one block—okay, maybe three or four, I wasn't counting—from the post office, he'd gotten himself lost.

I don't know if I was more scared for him, being lost, or for me, being in big trouble. I retraced my steps, looked on every corner, and walked slowly back up the street, checking each store: The Darling Shoppe, Newberry Five and Ten, The Feed Bag, Millie's Millinery, Fogarty's Appliances, where a crowd of small boys was watching puppets argue on a television set in the window.

Normally I would have stayed to watch too, because we didn't seem likely ever to have a television in our house. My father said it was too expensive and just a passing fad. I told him that I'd read in *Life* magazine that one out of seven families in America had a television set. He said I should count six houses down the street from us and go watch *their* set.

I examined the television-watching boys closely. No Artie.

"Seen a little boy dressed for church?" I asked the people I passed. No one had.

Just as I was about to give up and call a policeman, I saw

a commotion across the street. I ran over, hoping the hub-bub was about a little lost boy.

Where a building had been going up for months behind a tall fence was now the largest grocery store I had ever seen. *Piggly Wiggly Supermarket,* a banner said. A giant pig with huge golden scissors was cutting a ribbon strung across the front door, signaling the official opening of the store. And there pulling on the pig's curly tail was Artie.

"Artie!" I said, grabbing him. "I was scared to death. Don't ever wander away like that again!"

"He's okay, miss," the pig said. "I was watching him for you." I could see a man's face through the holes in the mask cut for breathing.

"Thank you," I said to the pig. I had never imagined having an occasion to say thank you to a pig. But there it was: *"Thank you," I said to the pig.* "Let's go, Artie," I said, reaching for his hand.

"No. I want to go in there."

"Artie, that's enough. We have to go home."

"No!" Artie ran into the market.

I collared him by the soap flakes and grabbed his hand.

"What is this place?" he asked, looking around.

I looked too. Soft music came from somewhere above. Ceiling lights reflected off the shiny metal of the shopping carts, and the red linoleum floors gleamed. "It's like a grocery store in Heaven," I said. Artie and I walked up and down the brightly lit aisles of peanut butter and rye bread, Twinkies and Oreos and Stopette deodorant, chops and steaks and bacon in tight plastic packages.

Pyramids of lettuce and oranges and beets in bright colors looked like paintings by some great fruit artist. "Buy me an apple, Francine. This apple," Artie said, taking an apple from the very base of the pyramid.

"No, Artie," I said, too late, as the pyramid collapsed and all the apples fell to the floor. "Come on, " I said. "Let's scram before they figure out it was us."

We were headed for the door when Artie stopped in front of a phone booth. "I want to check for nickels," he said, climbing onto the seat.

"Come *on*," I said, pulling his hand.

"Noooo!" cried Artie, grabbing onto the dial of the telephone and holding on tight. And then he wailed, "Franseeeeen, get me outa here!" His finger was stuck in the dial. I tried pulling it free, but it just got stuck tighter and tighter and Artie wailed louder and louder. People stopped to watch us, a red-faced girl and a little boy hanging by his finger from the telephone dial.

"Let me try," said a man in a blue jacket that had *Leroy, Manager* embroidered on the pocket. He opened a jar of Vaseline and smeared some on the dial and Artie's finger. A few tugs and the finger came free.

Leroy, Manager, was shaking with the laughter he was too polite to let out. "Thank you, Mister Leroy," I said, and hurried Artie away. My arm hurt from yanking on Artie and my face burned with humiliation. And Sophie thought I wouldn't like being an only child. Ha! Not today.

"Now don't go telling Mother any of this," I said once we were outside. "Do you hear me?" I looked at Artie's face. He would be telling Mother before the front door slammed behind us.

After all that, I was happy to spend my nickels to go home on the bus. Artie slept, his head bobbing against my shoulder, glasses sagging. He had a smile on his face and Rice Krispies stuck to his fingers. I pushed his glasses back up onto his nose.

What a day. What a lot of stuff for Artie to tell Mother. He snored softly, and I rested my head on his, breathing in the familiar warm, salty, little-boy smell.

We got off the bus at the stop near the Petrovs' store. Tiny, red-haired Mrs. Petrov was washing the front windows. I could see smeared red paint saying *Russkies go home* and a big six-pointed star on the glass. When she saw us, she shook her head. "That's why Petrov and I left Russia, to get away from such thugs," she said. "And now look, they follow us here. Russia explodes an atom bomb and it's our fault?"

Russia? Atom bomb? Where? Were people dead? Were we at war? I took Artie's hand and ran home, my face turned to the sky, watching for Russian planes loaded with bombs for Palm View Drive.

"Mama," Artie cried as we ran in the door, "Francine losted me and a telephone tried to eat me and—"

His shouts were drowned out by my own. "Mother. Mother!" I called, letting the screen door slam behind me.

"In here, Francine," she said from the kitchen, "and don't be so noisy."

The kitchen smelled of dish soap and coffee, familiar

and comforting. My mother and father were sitting at the table. She was clipping penny-off coupons from a magazine. Artie climbed into her lap and snuggled down.

I sat down too. "I just saw Mrs. Petrov. She said something about Russia dropping an atom bomb. Is that true?"

My father rustled his newspaper. "I was just reading it here. It was a test. Soviet scientists have successfully tested an atomic bomb." He shook his head. "Communist Russia with the bomb. That Mao fellow and his communist army in China. Commies fighting the French in Indochina. The world is getting a whole lot more dangerous."

All I knew about communists was that they believed everyone owned everything in common, wore fur hats, and hated God and America. Now they had an atom bomb. My stomach fell between my knees, or at least that's what it felt like. "Will they drop the bomb on us?"

My father leaned over and ruffled Artie's hair with one big hand and mine with the other. "Now, don't you little guys start worrying. You got the U.S. government, your mother, and me. We won't let anything bad happen to you."

I got up to leave the kitchen but stopped and turned back. "Oh, I just remembered. Somebody painted nasty stuff on the Petrovs' window."

"Oh, poor Luba," my mother said. "I have to call her."

"Stay out of it, Lorraine," said my father.

"Why would someone do that?" I asked him. "The Petrovs aren't communists, are they?"

"Someone who'd do that wouldn't care what's true and what's not," he said. "They just want to stir up trouble. You stay out of it too, Francine. Get groceries at Willard's Market for a while."

"But I like—"

"That's enough, Francine," my mother said. "Listen to your father."

I went to my room and lay on the bed. In a way, things had been simpler during the war. We all knew who the enemy was and worked together to defeat him. My father wasn't in the army—his eyes were bad and his feet were flat—but my mother had a victory garden, where she grew our vegetables so that more food could be sent to the soldiers. I liked to read lying on the warm ground under the tomato vines, smelling the pungent scent of the leaves and watching the pole-bean shadows dance on my legs. We ate lots of macaroni and fish, and I helped Dolores collect gum wrappers so the government could use the silver foil in the war effort.

And when it was all over, people hugged each other and danced with strangers, knowing the bad guys were gone and the good guys had made us safe. People's fathers and brothers and uncles came home, and we had plenty of meat again, and butter and gasoline and shoes. Was that all over now? Would Russia having the bomb mean another war and more dead soldiers?

I knew what atomic bombs could do. I had seen Fox Movietone newsreels of Japanese cities turned to rubble, of exploding buildings, children on fire, piles and piles of charred bodies. And the world was getting *more* dangerous. I pulled the blankets over my head.

6

Discovering Irony

"In order to make our writing livelier," Sister Basil said as we opened our grammar workbooks, "we can employ a number of tools. You know about adjectives and adverbs, phrases and clauses. Today we will learn about some figures of speech: similes, metaphors, oxymorons, and irony."

I already knew about similes, saying things were like other things, and metaphors, saying things *were* other things. Oxymorons, which used two words of opposite meaning together, and irony, where the ordinary meaning of the words is the opposite of what is really in your mind, were new to me.

We had to make up examples in our workbooks to show we understood. I wrote:

Simile: *Dolores blew her nose, which was as red as a rose.*

Metaphor: *When his cap pistol broke, the little boy cried a river of tears.*

Oxymoron: *I gave a silent cry of desperation.*

Irony: *I just love to go to the doctor for a shot.*

Irony was especially appealing to me. I thought of lots more examples, but I didn't write them down: *I was so pleased to see Mary Agnes Malone there. Yes, Mother, I think Dad looks exactly like Montgomery Clift. Sure, let's draw flowers all over our uniform skirts. I know Sister would be crazy about it. Oh, no, the idea of the world blowing up doesn't bother me one bit.*

I was pretty excited. With irony I could mean the very opposite of what I said, but no one would know that. I could say exactly what I thought without getting into trouble.

"Francine," Sister said, "will you please go up to the board and write down your example of a metaphor?"

"I can't think of anything I'd rather do," I said ironically.

After school I went to the classroom that served as the school library.

"Sister Peter Claver," I said to the nun reading behind the desk, "I'm Francine Green. Sister Basil the Great sent me to help you." *Sister Basil the Great*—was that irony or oxymoron? I wondered.

Sister Peter Claver, the librarian, was new this year. She looked up at me so quickly that her cheeks wobbled. "Hello, Francine. Call me Sister Pete. Most of the girls do."

I nodded.

"Thank you for coming," she said. "I could certainly use your help. But tell me, is this something you chose to do, or did Sister Basil request that you do so?"

Request? Sister Basil never requested. She had said, "You, Francine, go help Sister Peter Claver in the library after school." And what could I say but "Yes, Sister"?

"Some of both, I guess," I told Sister Pete. "I do like books."

"Well, then, welcome to the library, Francine Green." She stood up slowly, a great wave breaking on the shore of her desk (metaphor). Sister Pete in her black habit was as round as a bowling ball (simile), rolling around the library as she showed me the filing system for library cards, pointed out the shelving cart, and taught me how to check books in and out using the little rubber date stamp.

"Well, that wore me out," she said with a sad smile (oxymoron) as she sat back down at her seat behind the counter. I picked up a book to shelve: *Dotty Dimple at School*? Ye gods. No doubt a book full of deep wisdom (irony).

"Wait a moment, Francine. I'd like to get to know you a little bit. Why don't you tell me about some of those books you like?"

I didn't know how to talk to a nun except to say "Yes, Sister" and "No, Sister." What could I say to her? "Ummm" is what I said, and I looked down at my feet.

"Do you know this one?" She held up *Little Women*.

"Yes," I mumbled. "I liked that. And *Heidi*. *Stuart Little*. And . . ." My mind went blank and I couldn't think of another title. My face flamed.

Finally Sister Pete took pity on me. "Go ahead and shelve those books now, Francine. We'll talk another time. And thank you for your help."

I shelved books for a while, wondering while I worked where I could get a quarter for the movies on Saturday. Movie prices were sky-high (metaphor) and I was broke.

Wouldn't it be wonderful, I thought, if there were a library that had movies instead of books? You could check one out, take it home, open the covers, and the movie would play. Now, that would be even better than television.

I sighed and went on shelving: *The Runaway Sardine. Jean Craig Grows Up. Patriotic Plays and Pageants for Young People. Stories of Virgin Martyrs for Girls.* Ye gods.

I picked up a book with a blue cover. Someone was lucky enough to have just read *A Tree Grows in Brooklyn.* I had seen the movie a couple of years before, and then I had read the book for a book report in the sixth grade. The book was a lot longer, but both were great. Francie Nolan seemed so real. I liked how she survived and grew in a hard world just like the tree outside her window.

I didn't like how her father drank so much. He didn't just have martoonies at dinner. He would not go to work and spent all their money getting falling-down drunk. My father was pretty boring and didn't listen to me much, but at least he wasn't bad news like Mr. Nolan.

I understood when Francie felt alone sometimes, but I didn't know why she was so nice to her mother when her mother clearly loved her little brother better and let him go to school but made Francie work in a paper-flower factory.

I liked how she was strong and brave even though she was mostly obedient and didn't like to get into trouble. I wondered how she managed it.

I liked that her name was like mine.

By now I'd read everything worth reading in our library, and there was nothing left for me but *Nanette of the Wooden*

Shoes, Great Moments in Catholic History, and biographies of every saint God ever made. I'd read *Stuart Little* over and over, and the public library was too far away for me to walk from with an armload of books. I wondered if my father or Wally would drive me.

And I wondered if Francie was happy when she grew up.

Walking home, I passed Twentieth Century Fox. As usual, no movie stars were sitting on top of the fence, waiting for me. It was frustrating to live so near and yet so far. I knew movie stars were in there, but I had never seen one.

They would have known what to say to Sister Pete. Actors always knew what to say. No matter the problem or situation, movie actors had the right words and weren't afraid to speak up. If I were an actress, I would never be at a loss for words. But the reality was:

Metaphor: *Francine's tongue was tied in knots.*

Simile: *Sometimes Francine's brain is as empty as a barrel.*

Oxymoron: *Hear the loud silence of Francine Green.*

And irony: *How proud we are when we are able to use what we learn in class in our real lives.*

7

Fifteen Flavors of Butterfat

"Mother, we're going to Riley's for sodas," I called, linking arms with Sophie at the front door.

"Me too. Take me too." Artie, of course.

"No, Artie, you stay here," I said, giving him a little push. I was not about to suffer another outing with Artie so soon. "Be a good boy and I'll bring you a comic book."

"Donald Duck?" he asked.

I much preferred Archie—a lot of what I knew about being a teenager I learned from Betty and Veronica—but I nodded. "Donald Duck." Artie trotted off.

"Francine Louise Green! Where do you think you're going?" my mother asked from the kitchen door.

"I told you—to Riley's."

"Not like that you aren't."

I looked down: an old white shirt of my father's, blue jeans rolled up to the knee, and saddle shoes fashionably grimy. Very respectable. "What's wrong?"

"Your shoes are in desperate need of a polish." She shook her head. Jeepers, I heard her crowd ate goldfish when they were my age.

I could see Sophie trying to suppress a smile. Lucky Sophie, who didn't have to suffer maternal torments. I sighed. "Mother, all the girls wear—"

"Francine Green, you are not 'all the girls.' You are my daughter, and my daughter polishes her shoes. And combs her hair." I gave my shoes a quick polish while Sophie rolled her eyes, and finally we were on our way to Riley's.

Mr. Riley's nephew, Gordon, was working at the soda fountain after school and Saturdays, and I had heard he was downright swoony. We were going to see for ourselves.

Hot winds blew smoke over the city. The skies were darkened by the gray haze that burned my eyes and my throat.

"There's a fire somewhere," Sophie said.

"Big one," I added.

We pushed open the glass door of Riley's, breathed in the sweet scent of face cream, hair tonic, and hot fudge, and headed first for the magazine rack. My heart clenched like a fist when I saw the news magazines with pictures of the mushroom cloud of an atomic bomb on their covers. What if that were not smoke outside but the radioactive fallout from an atomic bomb? What would we do? How long would we have to live? What would I be thinking right now? I swallowed hard.

Sophie nudged me. "Look at that," she said, pointing to the new *Silver Screen*.

I looked, grateful for the distraction. "Five pages of photos of Montgomery Clift," screamed a yellow banner across the cover, "the talented young actor the teenagers call drooly and dreamy!" We read the whole magazine before putting it back on the rack.

"Let's see this Gordon Riley now," I said, ready to be dazzled. We hurried past the aspirin and Band-Aids to the jukebox in the corner. You could see the soda fountain from there. I put a nickel in the jukebox and pushed G7, "Nature Boy" by Nat King Cole. We swayed slowly to the music as we looked over our shoulders toward the soda fountain.

Susan Murphy's drippy brother, Scooter, was sitting on a stool, talking to a gorgeous guy in a white soda-jerk hat. Gordon Riley. Jeepers, he *was* swoony, with those waves in his hair, his little pink ears, and his dark eyes. He looked a little like a teenaged Montgomery Clift and a little like Joe Palooka, that handsome boxer from the comics. Sophie and I walked over and took seats at the counter.

"Your usual ice cream, now," the dreamboat was saying to Scooter, "is twenty percent butterfat, but Uncle Frank insists on twenty-two percent. That's what makes Riley's ice cream so good. Butterfat." He leaned over and began scooping ice cream out of the cooler into a dish. I wished I had all the money in the world so I could order gallons of ice cream and thousands of double hot fudge sundaes just to watch the dreamy way the veins and muscles in his arm moved. He set the dish of ice cream in front of Scooter, leaned on the counter, and said, "Did you know that it takes seven quarts of milk to make four quarts of ice cream?" Scooter shook his head and began to eat.

Gordon looked up then and noticed us. He came right over and asked, "What'll it be, glamourpusses?"

"Two root beer floats," said Sophie. "With chocolate ice cream."

Gordon nodded and began scooping out ice cream again. I kept my eyes on his arm.

He poured in the root beer and put the glasses down in front of us. Looking right into my face, he said, "Do you know that chocolate is the second most popular flavor in the U.S.A.? Vanilla is first. Think of that. Plain old vanilla. That's what people like. Vanilla. No imagination." He began to clean the counter with a damp rag. "If I were making ice cream, I'd make more flavors than Heinz has pickles. Ten flavors, maybe. Or fifteen. Think of it—not just chocolate, vanilla, and strawberry, but fifteen different flavors."

"Is that all you know about? Ice cream?" Sophie asked, slurping up the last of her root beer. My tongue lay in the bottom of my mouth like a wet towel.

"No sirree bob," said Gordon. "I know lots of things, like how to feed a jukebox, tune a jalopy, and treat pretty brown-haired girls with shy smiles." He winked at me.

"Oh nausea. Let's go, Francine."

On the way home, Sophie said, "He likes you."

My heart did a jitterbug. "No, he doesn't. He's just a flirt."

"Yes, and he was flirting with you."

I sighed. "He's so drooly!"

"He's a know-it-all. Ice cream. Who cares?" She took my arm. "Come on over for dinner."

"Thanks, but I can't. I have to go home." Really I just wanted to be alone and remember the veins on Gordon's arms and the way his lips got all red and pouty when he said "butterfat."

8

Searching for a New, Popular Francine

"I'll just die if I don't get a car for my birthday," Dolores said as we got ready for bed.

"Don't hold your breath," I told her. "On my last birthday I got underwear and a jigsaw puzzle of Saint Peter's in Rome. Remember? I sure don't see a car in your future."

"But I'll just die. All the most popular girls have cars." Dolores was very popular. She was obviously the right person to ask about what was on my mind.

She must also have been quite distracted thinking about that car, because she actually let me sit on her bed. I pushed aside her *Seventeen* magazine. *Fun with Ham,* it said on the cover, and *Are You Ready for Romance? A Quiz.* Well, I didn't know if I was ready for ham, but romance? Absotively. "Dolores, can I ask your advice?"

She put down her hairbrush and stretched. "And why would I help a dishrag like you? I have problems of my own."

"But that's it, Dolores. I *am* a dishrag. How will I ever get a boy to like a pathetic wet dishrag like me?"

"A boy, huh?" She sat down next to me. "It's about time. Let's see. Well, boys like to date popular girls."

"Of course, but how does an ordinary person like me go about getting popular?"

She looked at me closely and frowned a little. I could see her thinking. Thinking was very hard for Dolores. She read somewhere that it led to wrinkles, so she tried not to do it very often. Finally she said, "You could try to be more like the popular girls in your class."

Popular girls? What if that included the Perfect and Admirable Mary Agnes Malone? I would *die* before I would be like Mary Agnes Malone, and then Dolores and I could be buried together when she didn't get her car. I thought for a moment longer. "Susan Murphy is the most popular, I guess." She was the prettiest girl in the whole school.

"Well, watch her. Try to do what she does. Or watch me," Dolores continued. "You could do worse than be like me." She flipped her hair back with a graceful movement of her head and laughed a laugh that sounded like silver bells and hiccups.

I tossed my head and laughed like someone choking on fruitcake.

"Practice," Dolores said, frowning. "Then, once you're popular, you can get any boy you want."

"How? Specifically how do I do that?"

"Well, honestly," she said, "haven't you learned anything at all in thirteen years? Pick a boy. Find out about what he likes and say you like it, too. Go all goggle-eyed about horsepower and motor oil. Memorize the names of some ball teams. Tell him you always wanted to learn to fish or something."

I was about to ask Dolores if that would work with ice cream and butterfat, but she was just getting warmed up. "Never criticize him. Or disagree with him. And don't ever express your own opinion. And—"

"Jeepers," I said. "It sounds like Catholic school, only worse."

"Well, no one is born popular. You have to work at it. Wear the right clothes, be friends with the right people, join the right clubs, and comb your hair once in a while."

"Sophie says I should just be myself."

Dolores's eyes opened so wide, they looked like they'd pop right out of her head. "Yourself? Why would you want to do that?" She stood up slowly, straightened her skirt, and pulled her Sloppy Joe sweater way down. Then she walked slowly to the door, where she stopped, looked at me over her shoulder, and winked.

Holy cow. I couldn't see any boy not following her any- where after that. I'd have to keep Dolores away from the soda fountain at Riley's Drugs for sure.

The next day I started right in to be the new, popular Francine. I pulled the fuzz balls off my navy uniform sweater and rubbed dirt into my saddle shoes. The white blouse that I ironed pulled tight across my chest. Shrunk in the wash. I shrugged and buttoned my sweater up over it. It would have to do.

I'd pin-curled my hair the night before, but still it hung there, bangs to my eyebrows, parted in the middle and tucked behind my ears, limp and messy. What was I to do?

After school I asked Dolores. "Well, you could go to Maxine's World of Beauty for a permanent wave," she said.

"What will that do?"

"It'll curl your hair right up. They wrap the hair in metal curlers attached to wires and then plug them into—"

"Ye gods. I don't want to be electrocuted."

She took a clump of my hair in her hand and examined it. "It's not a bad color—kind of like maple syrup—but so stringy. Why don't we try my curling iron? Mom took Artie shopping for school clothes, so we can use the kitchen.

"Watch me," she said, taking a silver metal tongs-like thing and heating it on the burner of the stove. She twirled strands of her hair around the wand and finished up with a head full of ringlets.

"Now you." She turned the back of my head into curls before running off for a ride with Wally. I was on my own.

I heated up the iron again and wrapped my hair around it. "Yow," I cried, dropping the iron and sticking my burned finger in my mouth. I smeared butter over the burn and started again.

The butter made my hand all slippery, so it was hard to get the hair wrapped and unwrapped. I scorched my head a few times. My hair crackled and smoked. I smelled a little like a fire in the dog pound, but I could feel curls in my hair, so I kept at it.

Between curlings I reheated the iron. I guess it got too

hot, because when I rolled my bangs, pieces of hair cracked off and floated around my face. Ye gods.

I locked myself in the bathroom. My face in the mirror looked unfamiliar, with the curls in back and short, broken hair standing straight up in front. Pulling on the broken hair didn't help. Wetting it made it worse. This was the new, popular Francine, this greasy-faced wretch with a crewcut? I was miserable.

After crying for a while, I took a short nap, worn out from my efforts, and then tried to fix things up a bit. My hair was wavy in some places, kinky and crackly in others, and very short in front, but at least it wasn't limp and stringy anymore. I went in to dinner only a little bit nervous.

DINNER AT THE GREENS', Part 2

FATHER: Good Godfrey, what is that smell? *(He picks up his plate and sniffs it.)*

ARTIE: Look at Francine. She burned all her hair off! Fran-seeeeen is baaaaalllld!

MOTHER: Francine, what have you done to your hair?

FRANCINE: Dolores and I curled it. What do you think?

DOLORES: It's very stylish. Except for the front. *(Frowning)* Maybe a little sailor hat, tilted over your forehead, until it grows out.

FATHER: You look like a chicken with its feathers singed off.

MOTHER *(to Francine)*: Never mind, dear. It will grow
back and be nice and straight again.

FATHER *(muttering into his soup)*: A singed chicken . . .

Fade out

I took to wearing my school beanie pulled down low
over my forehead. I might have had to sport a crewcut, but
I didn't have to flaunt it.

I even wore the beanie in class. It was the only kind of
hat allowed, as if beanies were holy or something. I told
Susan and Gert and Florence that it was a new fashion, the
beanie tipped low over the face. "You know how interested
I am in fashion," I told them ironically. Funny thing,
Florence and a couple of other girls started wearing their
beanies the same way. Sister pushed them back on our heads
when she passed our desks, but we just pulled them forward
again after she'd gone by. Imagine, the new, popular
Francine—a trendsetter.

9

November 1949

Sophie's Speech
and Francine's Unplumbed Depths

"Come and help me find something to wear tonight," Sophie said when I came to the telephone. She had written a speech for a citywide contest on the topic "What Today's Youth Can Learn from Yesterday's Saints," sponsored by Los Angeles Catholic Youth, and tonight she was saying it out loud in front of students and parents from the whole city.

Sister Basil's face got scrunched and red when she heard that Sophie of all people had been chosen to speak, and the other girls started referring to her as "Sophie Bowman, that shining example of Catholic Youth." I recognized that—it was irony.

Sister Peter Claver seemed fine about Sophie being picked, and she began coaching her in the library after school. Every Monday, Wednesday, and Friday, while I shelved books about elves and horses and dead popes, I heard about the Blessed Martin de Porres of Peru.

"'I have chosen to speak about the Blessed Martin de

Porres,'" her speech began, "'even though he is not a saint yet. I think what is important about him is not whether or not he was canonized but that he helped people who needed help, and I don't think he would care if he were an official saint or not. That is one of the best things about him.'"

"But Sophie," I said when she had told me whom she'd chosen, "don't you think you should pick a holy saint who is important, one who performs miracles and has weeping sores on his body and can talk to God?"

"Do you think that's what makes someone a saint?" she asked me.

You could tell that Sophie didn't know much about saints. "Well, sure. Do *you* know anyone who performs miracles and talks to God?"

"I think there are different kinds of saints. Listen." She cleared her throat. "'Martin de Porres was born in Peru in 1579, the son of a Spanish knight and a Negro woman. His father was disappointed that the boy looked like a Negro, and he left the family. At twelve, Martin became an apprentice to a barber surgeon who cut hair and also operated on people.

"'He left when he was fifteen to become a holy brother in a monastery. He worked there as a barber and a gardener, spending his nights in prayer and his days caring for the poor and those stricken with plague, especially the slaves brought to Peru from Africa, even though that wasn't an easy thing to do in those days. He helped found a hospital, an orphanage, and a home for homeless dogs and cats. He even forgave the rats and mice that stole his food, saying that the poor little things were hungry.'"

"But anybody could do those things," I said. "Why, Christina the Astonishing could fly, and Saint Simon Stylites lived for forty-eight years on the top of a pillar, and Saint Bernadette had actual conversations with the Blessed Virgin. How come you didn't pick one of them?"

"Because I'm supposed to pick a model for today's youth. Do you think we should be encouraged to fly or live on a pillar?"

I thought a moment. "Of course not, but—"

"Martin de Porres did things that anyone could do to help people. That was his way of honoring God. That's why I chose him. Let me finish my speech.

"'We do not call Martin de Porres blessed because he withdrew from the world to fast and pray or beat himself with whips and chains or turned his bathwater into beer like some saints, but because he cared for those in trouble, like slaves and sick people and hungry mice. He gave food to those who needed food and a home to those who had none. He did not care about money or fame but only about what he could do for others. That is why we call him blessed.

"'And that is why we young people should learn from him, to be as kind and generous and compassionate as he was, not to judge people by the color of their skin or the size of their bank accounts, to stand up and do what is right when we know it is right.

"'The Blessed Martin de Porres died in 1639 of a fever, but in a way he never died, for he is still an inspiration to young people today and a shining example of social justice.'"

My head was spinning. I had never thought about saints quite like that, as human beings like me who did good things and tried to make the world a better place. Trust old Sophie to make me see things in a different way.

Later I wondered what saint I would have chosen to speak about. I considered roasted and tortured martyrs, miracle workers, hermits who lived in the desert on dry bread and bugs, but finally settled on Joan of Arc, who led the soldiers of France against the English invaders, even though she was just a peasant girl and afraid. Last year Ingrid Bergman starred in a movie about Saint Joan, which my parents let Dolores and me go see. I fell asleep, the movie being mostly talk and me being only twelve, but I knew about Saint Joan from religion class.

She was just an ordinary person like me at first, but then she saw something that needed doing and did it. Okay, not like me at all. But that's who I would have chosen. Probably.

By the time the big day came, I knew Sophie's speech well enough to deliver it myself, although the very thought made my stomach flutter alarmingly.

I put on my beanie, pulled it low on my forehead, and went over to Sophie's. Clothes were flung all over her room. Socks hung from dresser drawers, skirts and sweaters tumbled off the bed, and a white scarf patterned with four-leaf clovers dangled from the light fixture in the ceiling. "It looks like an explosion hit the Broadway's Junior Miss department," I said.

"Shut up and help me," Sophie said. "What should I wear? This? Or maybe this?" She held up a flowered dress and a blue nylon blouse.

"No," I said. "Your yellow sweater set. It's dreamy. And your dark-green pleated skirt."

She fished them out, tried them on, and twirled around the room. "Sit," I ordered her, "and I'll make sure the skirt covers your knees. You know how nuns are about knees."

The skirt passed the nun test. Sophie added saddle shoes over white socks that bagged around her ankles, and I tied a green ribbon in her hair. "You look gorgeous," I said, "and you're smart and well prepared. Don't worry."

"I'm not worried," she said. "I know my speech is good. But I didn't want to look like a poor relation at that snooty school."

We went outside to wait for Mr. Bowman, who would drive us downtown. Bitter brown smoke came through the kitchen window. "What's that awful smell?" I asked Sophie. "Is your father cooking?"

She sniffed. "My father's friend Jacob Mandelbaum must be here. He smokes stinky black cigars."

"Is he coming with us?"

"No, he's going to see the Hollywood Stars play baseball."

"You mean the team or actual movie stars?"

"You're kidding, right?"

"Right, Sophie."

"I can't always tell," she said. "I'm not that great in the sense of humor department." I gave her hand a squeeze, meaning *I know, but you're my best friend anyway.*

Mr. Bowman drove us to Holy Cross in Beverly Hills, where the speech contest would take place. It *was* a snooty school, much larger and fancier than All Saints, with its own chapel. A sort of Holier-Than-Thou Cross, I thought.

Sophie gave us a little wave as she went up and joined the other speakers on stage. Mr. Bowman searched for seats for us and then, bowing slightly, said, "After you, Miss Green." We sat.

Suddenly I felt shy. I didn't know what to say to him. He was so old and smart, a real writer and all. We sat in silence for an uncomfortably long time. Finally he said, "How was school today, Francine?"

Ah, good. A question I knew how to answer. "Fine," I said. More silence. I cleared my throat. "And how was work?"

He smiled. "Fine," he said. "But we were talking about you. Do you have a favorite class?"

"English," I said. "Recently we learned about irony and oxymorons." There was more silence. "And we read a poem about the ocean having 'unplumbed depths.' Don't you love that—unplumbed depths? It sounds so quiet yet full of possibilities."

Mr. Bowman was looking at me solemnly. Maybe I had talked too much. My cheeks grew hot. "I'm glad you're friends with my Sophie," he said. "She's a puzzle to me—so much spunk and so little common sense, so much energy and so little imagination. She needs someone like you."

She does? Need me? Doesn't he know it's the other way around? "I'm glad Sophie's my friend too," I said finally. "I learn lots of things from her, like about free speech and improving the world and not being so afraid of trouble. I guess we make a good pair."

"Best friends," he said.

"Best friends," I agreed.

The auditorium had filled up with relatives and friends of the students on the stage. There were some priests there, too, but no sisters. Nuns don't get out much.

The Perfect and Admirable Mary Agnes Malone was one of the speakers, of course, and her mother sat in the seat behind me. She leaned forward. "Francine, dear," she said, "how nice of you to come and cheer on the more accomplished girls."

"Francine may surprise you one day, madam," said Mr. Bowman over his shoulder. "Like the ocean, she has unplumbed depths."

Me? I will? I do? I gave Mrs. Malone a smile full of depth and turned back toward the stage.

Sophie looked so small up there. She twirled a lock of her hair and tucked it behind an ear.

I thought she would have a better chance of winning if she were either the first speaker or the last, but her place was right in the middle of the group. It didn't matter. She won anyway. She got a fake gold cup with two handles and "First Place, Catholic Youth Speech Contest, 1949" engraved on it. Mr. Bowman hugged Sophie and then me, and I hugged them back.

Walking to the car, Mr. Bowman held Sophie's hand and swung it as he sang some big, loud song in a language

I didn't recognize. "German," Sophie said. "Beethoven. 'Ode to Joy.' It's his happy song."

"What would you say to a strawberry sundae?" Mr. Bowman asked us.

Sophie and I called out in chorus, "Hello, sundae!"

"But can we stop at the convent first?" Sophie asked him. "I promised Sister Pete I'd bring the trophy over to show her if I won."

I was a little worried. It was probably just a silly rumor, but I'd heard that nuns had their heads shaved, and I was afraid they relaxed by taking off their veils and running around bald, something I certainly did not wish to see.

The convent building next to the school was quiet and dark. Mr. Bowman waited in the car while Sophie and I knocked at the door. A fully veiled Pete opened at our first knock. Her big grin shone like a quarter moon in the dim light of the convent hall. "I knew you would do it," she said as she clapped Sophie on the back. "Well done, my girl."

Sister Basil joined us at the door. "This," she said, "will be a suitable addition to the school trophy case." She took the trophy from Sophie's hands.

"No, it's for my father's desk," Sophie said.

Sister Pete turned to Sister Basil. "I know it's customary for the trophies won by All Saints girls to stay together," she said, "but perhaps—"

"Yes, it is customary," said Sister Basil. "The trophies belong to the school." The convent door closed.

"That's not fair. It's mine," Sophie said, kicking the gravel path on the way to the car. "You're wrong, Sister Basil the Not-So-Great."

"Dead wrong, Sister Basil the Rotten," I added. We joined Mr. Bowman and went to drown our sorrows in strawberry sundaes.

10

Montgomery Clift!

I pounded on Sophie's door early Saturday morning. "Sophie," I called. "Come and look. Look, Sophie, look!"

I shook the newspaper at the door until it opened. A sleepy-looking Mr. Bowman said, "Come in with your earth-shaking news, Francine. Sophie is in the kitchen."

I galloped through the living room to the kitchen. "Sophie, Sheila Graham. Look. Monty. Here. Look. See."

Sophie swallowed a mouthful of cereal and put down her spoon. "Jeeps, Francine, you sound like a Dick and Jane reader," she said. "Sit down and breathe. Then tell me."

I sat down and panted for a while. Then I tried again. "In today's paper." I waved it at her. "In Sheila Graham's column. Tonight. At eight. A premiere." I took a gulp of air and tried to complete a sentence. "It's Monty's new movie, *The Heiress*. At the Carthay Circle Theater. He will be there. With his date, Elizabeth Taylor. Right here in Los Angeles!"

Sophie grabbed the paper and read the item. "Holy

smokes. You're right. But so what? Do you think they'll stop off and visit you?"

"No, but we could go visit them."

"Really?"

"Yes, really. Ordinary people go to premieres all the time. We can watch the stars get out of their limousines, and clap and cheer, and maybe get them to look at us."

"Let's do it," Sophie said.

"Yes, let's."

She looked at me quizzically. "You mean it? Sometimes you don't, you know."

"I know, but this is Monty. I'll do it. I really will. We just have to convince my parents and your father and get a ride somehow. Wally has his father's car on Saturday nights. Maybe he and Dolores'll take us." I jumped up. "I have to go home now and get ready."

"Francine, you goof, it's thirteen hours away," Sophie said.

"Thirteen hours? Is that all? I'll have to hurry. See you at six thirty?"

She nodded.

Mr. Bowman, in corduroys and an old felt hat, was pruning the roses that lined the front walk. "Got to hurry, Mr. Bowman," I shouted as I ran off. "Montgomery Clift is coming to see me!" He saluted, and I ran home.

"Of course not," Dolores said when I asked her about a ride. "People don't take their kid sisters on their dates."

"But this is really, really, really important," I said. "Name your price."

She looked at me. "Okay. Dishes for a week. And you'll write my next history paper."

"Done." And it was. At six thirty Wally, Dolores, and I picked up Sophie in his parents' yellow Packard. I had to wear the old beige dress I wore for church and visiting relatives, but I did have new black flats. And I wore a powder-blue beret of Dolores's over my forehead instead of my beanie. It had cost me another week of dishes.

I bounced and squealed in the backseat until Wally stopped the car. "Pipe down, squirt," he said, "or you're walking the rest of the way." I piped down.

People were already gathering when we got to the theater. "We're going to play miniature golf and catch a burger at the Kentucky Boys," Wally said as we got out of the car. "We'll pick you up at nine. Be ready or walk home."

Sophie and I pushed our way to the front of the crowd. "In only one hour Monty will be here," I told Sophie.

We read all the movie posters and then stood and stared for a while. "In only fifty-five minutes Monty will be here," I said.

We looked around, watched people walk down the street, and read the movie posters again. "In only fifty minutes Monty will be here."

"Jeeps, enough, Francine," Sophie said.

So we waited. And waited. By eight fifteen I could stand it no longer. "Did we miss them?" I asked no one in particular. "Or maybe they're not coming. Oh no, could it be they're not coming?"

"Take it easy, little girl," said an older woman behind me. "They're stars—they're never on time."

And sure enough, it was eight thirty before a limousine pulled up. I started to jump up and down and scream, but it was only Olivia de Havilland, who was in the movie with Monty. She got out and waved to the crowd, who cheered, except for me. I was saving my cheers for Monty.

A few minutes later another limousine came. Out stepped Elizabeth Taylor, gorgeous in white mink and a dress that looked like blue whipped cream. And behind her, standing on the same earth, in the same city, on the same block as Francine Green, was Montgomery Clift. In person.

He was so small and thin in his tuxedo, like he needed taking care of. I wanted to hold him and tell him it would be all right. My face grew hot, my heart pounded, and I had a funny, fluttery feeling in my stomach. Montgomery Clift. The actual Montgomery Clift, right in front of me. He waved once or twice to the crowd but mostly kept his eyes down. There was no smile on his beautiful face.

Women around us started jumping up and down, yelling, "I love you, Monty," and "Monty, look at me, Monty," and "Here, over here, Monty." Next to me Sophie, being Sophie, shouted, "Ban the bomb!"

Monty stopped walking and turned his head toward us. "He's looking at us!" I screamed. "Right at us!" And he was. At Sophie and at me. Montgomery Clift and I were attached, one on each side of his glance. I was overcome.

We rode home in silence, the way you do after church sometimes. Wally dropped Sophie off, and as soon as

Dolores and I got home, I climbed into bed. It had been a momentous day. I had seen Montgomery Clift. I wondered if he would remember me, if he was lying in bed that very moment thinking, "I wonder who that brown-haired girl in the blue beret and new black flats was." The thought made my heart pound and my stomach flutter. I knew I'd never get to sleep that night. In fact, I'd probably never sleep again. But it was worth it. I had seen Montgomery Clift and, even better, he had seen me.

11

Pink Underwear

"Sister Basil the Great," the Perfect and Admirable Mary Agnes Malone said, "Sophie Bowman was causing trouble while you were out of the room." When Sister was called away for a few minutes, she always left Mary Agnes in charge. And Mary Agnes always squealed on any girl who took a wrong breath or spoke out loud or shared her homework.

"Ah, the brazen Sophie Bowman," said Sister, shaking her head. "Do you know how close you are to the fires of Hell?"

Sophie stood up. "Does God really send people to Hell for asking questions? Because that's all I was doing—asking a question. About the religion homework. I wanted to know whether if you crossed the international dateline on a Friday morning and it changed to Saturday, you could then eat meat. And if you crossed the other way on Sunday, would you have to go to Mass again the next day? And if—"

Sister marched herself down the aisle and grabbed Sophie's hands. "Why are your hands red?"

"I dyed all my underwear red and the dye won't wash off my skin." Sophie grinned. "It was a protest against the mindless conformity of uniforms."

A chorus of snorts sounded, and Gert whispered, loudly, "What a weirdie!"

"You are flirting with danger, you foolish girl!" Sister said. "The communists, *the Reds,* are at this very moment destroying families, murdering priests, and preparing to invade our country, and you dye your underwear red. Do you want people to think you are a communist? Have you no sense?" Sister turned and examined the room. "You, Miss Mouse," she said to Florence Bush, "I don't have to keep my eye on you. Change seats with Miss Bowman. I want her right here where I can watch her."

Florence, her face flushed with embarrassment, took her books and her lunch bag and moved to Sophie's desk. Sophie sat down in Florence's former seat, the desk right in front of me. She stuck her red hand behind her and waggled "hello" at me.

Not ten minutes had passed when Sophie's hand waggled again. This time there was a folded piece of paper in it. I ignored her, but the waggling got more and more frantic, until I was sure both of us would be standing in the trash can, so I took the note from her hand.

Do you believe all that about communists killing priests and trying to take over our country? I don't think it's true. Do you?

I wrote an answer and stuck it in her hand: *I think com-*

munists are pretty scary, Soph, now they have the bomb and everything.

We have the bomb, too, she wrote. *Maybe they think we're pretty scary.*

A few minutes later a red hand waggled at me again. *Did Susan Murphy ever find out whether nuns wear black underwear?*

I don't know. She never said.

You told me to ask you my questions instead of Sister Not-So-Great, but fat lot of good you are. I'll just have to ask her.

No don't, I was writing when Sophie's hand popped up. "Sister, I was just wondering," she said.

Sister smiled.

The trash can was but a short walk from Sophie's new desk. I looked at the statue of the Virgin Mary in the corner. Her face was gentle but sad, not only for her son, Jesus, who suffered and died on the cross, but for poor Sophie in the wastebasket, the pagan babies in Africa, and all the rest of us, worrying about Hell and communists and bombs.

Sophie had to stay after school for the crime of laughing out loud in the bathroom (the Perfect and Admirable Mary Agnes Malone was bathroom monitor, of course, assisted by her sidekick, the weasely Weslia Babchuk). I took the bus home alone.

Before Sophie came, I was alone a lot. Oh, I wasn't a hermit or an outcast or anything. I always had someone to eat lunch with and play hangman with on rainy days. But I didn't have a best friend.

Sometimes I went home with Florence or had Mary

Virginia Mulcahy come to my house, and in the fourth grade my paper dolls and I suffered with Mary Agnes Malone, but I just didn't fit in with the other groups—not the wild girls or the pious ones or the Future Homemakers of America. I wasn't like them, and being different felt wrong, so I kept quiet about it.

In the third grade Margaret Mary Russell and I spent some Saturdays together at the children's matinee. My parents gave me a nickel for the movie and another one for popcorn and then dropped us off for the double feature. Margaret Mary's mother picked us up. Her father died in the war and I was not supposed ever to mention the war or dying or fathers to Margaret Mary. My mother said she was fragile.

When we were lining up for the May Day procession that year, Margaret Mary whispered to me, "The whole school smells like flowers. Sort of like how I imagine Heaven."

Sister Basil, passing by, grabbed Margaret Mary's arm and shook her. "You, girl, no talking in line!" Margaret Mary was so frightened that she peed, right there in line in the hallway. The pee ran down her legs and puddled on the floor.

Margaret Mary didn't come back to All Saints, and I went to the movies on Saturdays with Dolores, who complained that she was much too old for children's matinees, except once when the film for *My Pal Trigger* broke and we got to see Gregory Peck and Ingrid Bergman in *Spellbound* instead. I stayed out of Sister Basil's way after that, and I never, ever, talked in line.

But now I had Sophie. We agreed about so many things,

like uniforms, chocolate ice cream, and Dolores. We laughed at the same dumb stuff and hated the same people.

And the fact that we had one big difference didn't get in the way. I was a coward, and Sophie was brave. She didn't worry about getting in trouble and wasn't afraid of Sister Basil at all. I must admit I sort of enjoyed her standing up for herself and making trouble for Sister, as long as it didn't make any trouble for me.

When I was six or seven, during the war, I used to see posters pasted up warning people against leaking government secrets. One poster showed a sinking ship with the words *Loose Lips Sink Ships*. Another had a drowning soldier over the caption *Someone Talked*. I had nightmares for weeks afterward, worried that something I said had caused some poor soldier to drown. I didn't know just what a first grader could say to cause such a tragedy, but I took no chances. I just kept quiet. I guess it became kind of a habit.

During dinner that night I got a phone call from Sophie. "Big trouble, Francine," she said. "I'm under house arrest. Can't leave the house except for school and can't talk on the phone for two weeks. Two weeks!"

"You're on the phone now."

"That's because my jailer just went into the bathroom and took his newspaper. We have a few minutes."

"What happened?"

"My red underwear turned our laundry pink. Everything—sheets, towels, his undershirts and handkerchiefs—pink. You should see them hanging on the line. Pink."

I started to laugh, but she said, "Not funny, Francine!

I'm locked in the house with a very angry man in a pink undershirt who will make me read improving books and have serious conversations with him for *two whole weeks.* I will just die."

"Can I send you a care package, like people do for starving children?"

"Yes, yes. A Baby Ruth, some notepaper, and a bottle of root beer. Please."

"Okay, I'll—"

"Got to go. I just heard the toilet flush. Leave it in the bushes outside my window."

When I told my father what had happened at the Bowmans', he laughed. "This sure doesn't seem like a good time for a person to run around in a pink wardrobe," he said. "Pinkos aren't very popular right now."

Pinko. I knew that meant communist, like Red. I knew communists came from Russia and were people to be afraid of. I knew Sister thought they were evil and godless and would destroy our immortal souls as well as our country. Would people think Mr. Bowman was a communist because his undershirt was pink? Would he be arrested and sent to Russia? How long did pink dye stay in a person's clothes? And where would I get the money for a root beer *and* a Baby Ruth?

12

Changes

I took a deep breath before stepping into Riley's Drugs. My mother had sent me for bobby pins and aspirin. I was going to take the opportunity to flirt with Gordon Riley. My hair had grown out enough, so it looked like something someone might have done on purpose, but I checked my reflection in the glass door to make sure. I remembered all the things Dolores had told me and practiced asking questions about hot rods and butterfat as I walked to the back of the store.

The soda counter was nearly empty, except for Gordon, a trio of older ladies with their silver hair in hair nets, and a couple of boys shooting the papers from soda straws at the ladies. I took a seat at the end of the counter, my heart skipping and my stomach doing back flips. Gordon Riley and Montgomery Clift did that to me.

"Root beer float with chocolate ice cream, right?" Gordon said when he saw me. Sophie and I had been in lots of times for root beer floats with chocolate ice cream. Sophie always ordered for both of us. I had yet to exchange a word with Gordon myself.

My face grew hot. I nodded, and the root beer float appeared in front of me.

"I know your name is Francine," he said to me. "Mine's Gordon."

My bones were melting. I nodded and took a slurp of my root beer.

"You go to school around here?"

I shook my head and took another slurp.

"I'm at University High, a sophomore," he said. "You know anyone there?"

I shook my head again. Ye gods. I was such a droop. A dishrag, a sad sack, a dope. Gordon Riley was right there talking to me and I couldn't say a word. Just sat there with my face red, slurping up root beer. Ye gods.

A teenaged couple, holding hands, sat down, and Gordon went over to serve them. I kept slurping until the grating noise of the last drops echoed along the counter.

Someone grabbed me from behind and shouted, "Gotcha!" I jumped a mile into the air.

Gert Miller and Margie McGonigle slid onto the stools on either side of me. "Wow! You should have seen your face!" Margie shrieked. "What were you thinking about so hard?"

"Never mind," I said, pushing my empty glass away. "I'm leaving."

"No, stay," said Gert. "Sorry we scared you. C'mon, stay.

I'll buy you another root beer float." She called out to Gordon, "Three root beer floats, my good man, and don't skimp on the ice cream."

"We're drowning our sorrows," Margie said. "I was planning to have a slumber party over Christmas vacation, but my dad got a look at my report card." She cocked her head toward Gert. "And her mother drinks, you know, so we can't have it at her house." Gert nodded.

Our floats arrived, and we slurped in unison for a minute. "Hey," Margie said, "what if we have the party at your house?"

My house? I'd had birthday parties when I was little, but the girls had never come over for a slumber party before. I suppose that's because I'd never asked them. I never thought they'd want to come. "Really? Sure," I said. "I'll ask."

"Neat," said Margie.

"Swell," said Gert.

"Super," they said together.

I ran to Sophie's. She was finally off house arrest, thank goodness. I had to tell her about the party *right away*. It would be so great. We would dance and tell jokes and eat too much. The other girls would get to know Sophie, how much fun she could be when she wasn't trying to bother Sister or save the world from fascism. This *would* be super.

"Soph," I shouted, banging on the door until it opened. "Soph!"

"What is it?" she asked. "Is Montgomery Clift in town again?"

"Listen to this," I said, following her inside. "We're going to have a slumber party over Christmas vacation. I have to ask my parents, but I'm sure it'll be okay."

"What?"

"A slumber party. You know, where friends sleep over and make fudge and paint each other's toenails and dance."

"I hate fudge, I don't know how to dance, and my only friend is you. I won't come." She marched into her room with me on her heels.

"Come on. It'll be fun. Gert and Margie will be there, of course, and we'll invite Mary Virginia, Florence, and Susan."

"No, thanks."

I flopped onto her bed. "Why not?"

"Because they're your friends, not mine."

"They'd be your friends if you got to know them and let them get to know you."

Sophie grimaced at herself in the mirror. "They know me all right, and I know them, and we'll never be friends. Go have your silly party without me."

"Come on, Sophie, I wouldn't do that. We're best friends, but you could at least try to be friends with them, too. And you don't hate fudge."

"I would if Gert made it." Sophie brightened. "Hey, maybe we could have our own slumber party, just us. We could drink root beer and read movie magazines and gossip about the other girls."

"That's what we do all the time. I wanted this to be special, to do slumber party things." I could feel the excitement draining out of me like air out of a leaky old balloon. Why did Sophie have to be so stubborn?

Could I have the party without her? Would that really be all right? I looked over at her and she looked right back at me, pushing her hair back behind her ears. I couldn't desert her for Gert Miller. "I suppose we could have a party by ourselves," I said. "Gee, I can't wait to tell Margie and Gert that I'm having the slumber party but they can't come. That *will* be a fun conversation." I sat up on my heels. "If I agree to do it your way, *you* have to agree to do some special slumber party things. Like dance."

"I told you, I don't know how to dance," Sophie said, sitting on her desk.

"Of course you do. Everyone dances. You just move your feet, swing your hips, snap your fingers. Wait, I'll show you." I had never danced with an actual boy, but I cut a mean rug in front of the mirror in the bathroom.

I jumped up and switched on Sophie's radio. "Oh, goodie, it's 'Tiger Rag.'" The Mills Brothers crooned and tooted and thumped, "Hold that tiger! Hold that tiger! Hold that tiger! Hold that tiger!"

"Feel it, Sophie," I shouted over the music. "Here." I touched my ears. "And then here," I said, pointing to my stomach. "And then here, in your feet. And you're dancing."

"Francine, do you know how silly you look?"

"I do not. I'm jitterbugging. I'm supposed to look like this." I grabbed Sophie's hand. "Come on, let's boogie-woogie."

Sophie resisted as I tried to pull her up. "Let go. I don't

want to do this. I don't want to feel things in my stomach and my feet. Let go!" She jerked away and sat back on her desk.

"Sophie Bowman, sometimes I don't get you at all. Won't you even try?"

"Dancing is so ordinary. *Everybody* does it. *All girls* dance. I'm not ordinary, I'm not all girls, and I don't want to be."

"You could dance in an unordinary, spectacularly individual way. Come on and try."

I pulled her up and she moved around a little, her feet turning this way and that, her arms flailing as if she were chasing bees away. "Well, it's not pretty, but I think it's dancing," I told her.

She stopped. "That's enough," she said as she flopped onto her bed.

"I'm sorry I said that, Soph. You weren't doing so badly."

"I am not about to wiggle around and have people laugh at me. If I can't do it right, I just won't do it."

"What? The brave and fearless Sophie? Come on, take a chance." Holy cow, here I was telling Sophie to try, to risk a little, instead of the other way around. What a surprise.

"Listen, Soph, you won," I said. "We're not having the slumber party. But we *are* going to get you dancing. Now get off that bed and do what I do."

We stumbled around for a while to the music, and I think maybe Sophie enjoyed it a tiny bit although she said it was just plain hard work. "I have to stop now," I finally said. "My mother is waiting for her aspirin, and besides, my stomach hurts."

I started home at a run, but my insides kept cramping up. Food poisoning, I thought. Or more likely too many root beer floats.

But it wasn't. Changing for bed that night, I discovered why my belly hurt and my blouses were too tight. I had gotten what my mother called "your monthly visitor" and Dolores called "the curse." It must have been all the bouncing around at Sophie's.

My mother gave me a box of sanitary napkins, an elastic belt, and a booklet called "So You're a Woman Now" from the people who made Kotex. She brought me a cup of milky tea and stroked my hair. "You're getting so grown up," she said. "My little girl."

I sipped my tea and thought. I had always thought that growing up, like dying, was something that happened to other people. Not me. Yet here I was.

Getting my period seemed so final. It wasn't like hopscotch, where if you messed up, you could start again. Yesterday I was a kid, and today God poked me in the stomach and said, "You're grown up now, Francine. What are you going to do about it?" There was no going back.

After everyone was in bed, I called Sophie. "Soph," I whispered, "guess what! I'm bleeding. I got my period."

"Oh, ick. Poor you."

"I don't mind. It just means that I'm growing up. Dolores seems to handle it without too many problems." I looked down at my chest. "And it does mean cleavage, you know."

"Well, I'm never going to get my period."

"Sophie Bowman, for such a smart person, you're dumb sometimes."

"Who cares?" she said.

"Good night, Sophie."

"Good night, Francine."

13

December 1949

Meeting Jacob Mandelbaum

From way down the street Sophie and I could hear his voice, roaring and thundering like the sea. "How can you say Irv Noren is a better hitter than Frank Kelleher? What a lot of hooey. That Kelleher, he's such a slugger, he has muscles in his *hair*." The voice stopped roaring—to give someone else a chance to talk, I supposed—and then resumed. "Harry, my friend," it said, "you know baseball like you know cooking."

"That's Jacob Mandelbaum," Sophie said as we walked up the path to her porch, where Mr. Bowman and another man were sitting on lawn chairs.

"I didn't know your father liked baseball. I thought he was more of a serious opera kind of guy."

"He doesn't, but he likes Jacob Mandelbaum."

"Jacob," Mr. Bowman was saying as we climbed the stairs, "others obviously agree with me. Irv Noren was voted MVP of the Pacific Coast League for 1949. Most Valuable Player."

A man who looked like everybody's grandfather took a big cigar out of his mouth and said, "Feh, by me MVP means Most Visible *Punim*—a pretty boy who gets his picture in the papers. If you said Ozark Ike Zernial, maybe. That boy tore up the field. But I still think Frankie Kelleher, a California boy like me, is—"

"Mr. M, you're not from California," Sophie said, kissing him on the cheek. "This is my friend, Francine Green. Francine, meet Jacob Mandelbaum."

Mr. Mandelbaum stood up and bowed to me. "Sophie, darling, how did you do it, find the one girl in the whole world as beautiful as you?"

I blushed and sat on the porch railing. "Nice to meet you, Mr. Mandelbaum," I said.

He winked at me and sat down again. "Of course I'm a California boy, Sophie, my darling," he said. "Look at my driver's license: 445 Maple Avenue, Los Angeles 36, California. The great state of California says I'm a California boy. I am also a proud U.S. citizen, obey the law, pay my taxes, and fly the flag on the Fourth of July. A real Yankee Doodle and a California boy, that's me." He leaned back, and smoke swirled about his head.

"Mr. Mandelbaum is an actor," Sophie said to me. "In the movies. His movie-star name is Jack Mann."

A movie star? He didn't seem like a movie star, with his thin gray hair, sad brown eyes, and funny foreign talk, but my heart started to pound anyway. Did he, I wondered, know Montgomery Clift?

"Jack Mann. Feh. Mandelbaum, it means almond tree.

What does Mann mean? *Bubkes,* nothing." He leaned forward. "They say my real name is too foreign. Too Jewish, they think but don't say."

I cleared my throat. "I myself like *Mandelbaum* better," I said. "It sounds like part of a poem. But I suppose *Mann* is a better name for a movie star."

"Movie star, no. No kind of star. A character actor," he said, blowing smoke into the air. "That means small parts, tiny parts sometimes, but not even them much right now. The FBI doesn't like my causes or my friends, and my studio dances when the FBI plays the fiddle."

The FBI playing the fiddle? What was he talking about? I thought the FBI arrested bad guys and kept us safe.

"All the studios are cooperating with the FBI, Jacob," said Mr. Bowman. "And as to your causes and your friends, why, it's a bad time to support the communists. We keep hearing about Stalin's atrocities—"

"Joe Stalin, sure, he's a monster, with his labor camps and murder squads, but the communists don't have it *all* wrong. People are important, communism says, not property. People, peace, brotherhood, civil rights: When did these become dirty words? Communist words?" Mr. Mandelbaum stood up and ran his fingers through his hair, making it stand up like beach grass. "I've had it good in this country, Harry, and I want that for every person—enough to eat, a job, the freedom to speak, to work, to protest, to—" He stopped. "Bah. Actors. You give us a line and we make a speech. I apologize." He bowed slightly and sat down again.

I'd heard of Stalin, the evil communist dictator, but labor

camps and murder squads sounded awful. Communists must be worse than I thought, and here Jacob Mandelbaum was defending them. I'd never heard anyone have a good word for communists except Sophie, and I figured that was just Sophie being Sophie. Now there was Mr. Mandelbaum. I chewed on my lip and studied him. He didn't seem deluded or evil or stupid.

We were all quiet for a minute. Finally Sophie cleared her throat and said, "Francine knows all about actors and movies and movie stars, don't you, Francine?" She nudged me.

"Not *everything*," I said softly.

Mr. Mandelbaum stared at me solemnly, smoke circling his head. "You maybe want to act, Francine?" he asked.

"No, she's too chicken," said Sophie. "She wouldn't like everybody looking at her."

What did Sophie know? I looked down at my lap, embarrassed.

"Acting, you know, is like baseball," Mr. Mandelbaum said, puffing on his cigar. "Listen and I'll tell you."

Mr. Bowman laughed and said, "This sounds like a two-beer story, Jacob. Wait a minute and I'll get us another one."

Mr. Mandelbaum took a long drink of the new beer and wiped his mouth on his sleeve. "So," he said, "once Lefty Gomez—I think it was Lefty Gomez. Or Dizzy Dean. No, Lefty Gomez. So anyway, in this one game he was pitching, the right fielder—was it Butch Moran? No. Never mind—the right fielder was a bum. Couldn't catch the ball to save his soul. Every time a hitter hit to right field, this fielder would miss the ball, it would hit the fence and bounce off, and by the time he chased it down and threw to second base, a single had become a double, a double had become a triple. It happened one, twice, three times.

"The other team catches on. They start hitting every ball to right field and scoring runs off the fielder's mistakes, and still he can't catch the ball. Finally, Lefty, he gives the right fielder such a frown, like he's daring the guy to miss again." Mr. Mandelbaum leaped up. He twisted his face into the grouchiest of frowns and started twirling his arm like a windmill. "Lefty winds up and pitches. The batter swings. The ball flies into right field, goes right through the fielder's hands, and bounces off the fence. By the time he grabs it and throws it to third, another run scores.

"The ball comes back to Lefty. He's so angry, steam is coming out of his ears. He turns and stares at the right field-er. But the right fielder, his back is to Lefty. He's looking at the fence, examining it, like there's something wrong with the fence and that's the problem. Lefty, he's so mad, he winds up and throws the ball, not to the batter, but right at the Joe Knucklehead in right field. The throw is high, it hits the fence, just in front of the guy. The fielder, still staring at the fence, thinks it's a hit. This time he grabs it, spins, and sends a perfect throw to second base!" Mr. Mandelbaum grabbed at the air, spun, and mimicked a perfect throw. "Of course, there's no runner there. No runner anywhere. Everyone's laughing at the schmo in right field, and Lefty looks like he'll explode." He laughed until his cheeks were wet with tears. "No runner. What a schmo! True story."

We applauded noisily. Mr. Mandelbaum bowed to us, sat down, and puffed again on the awful black cigar.

"That's pretty funny, Mr. M," Sophie said, "but what does it have to do with acting?"

"It's like this," Mr. Mandelbaum said. "As long as you're nervous out there, worried about making the play, about people watching you, about making a mistake, you won't do it right, whether you're in right field or on a movie set. You have to relax and let the ball come to you. Forget you are bashful and people are looking. Just relax and let the magic come. That's baseball. And acting. Probably life, too."

I stared at Mr. Mandelbaum. He seemed twice as big as the rest of us, with his loud voice and wild ideas. Defending the communists? Comparing acting to baseball? I never heard such things before. I could see why Sophie and her father liked Mr. Mandelbaum despite the smelly cigar.

"'Just relax and let the magic come,'" said Sophie as she walked me home. "What does *that* mean?"

"I think I get it," I said. "It's like dancing."

14

Hammering the Nail Back into Place

Sometimes when she's really excited, Sister Basil spits when she talks, and the girls in the front row try to hide behind their books. I know that Saint Comgall worked miracles with his magic spit, but all Sister Basil does is speckle the books, so it was a relief to watch a film in class, even if it was pretty boring and had no movie stars. It was a lot better than ducking spit and listening to Sister Basil talk about teen martyrs.

Afterward we took class time to write a report on the film. I chewed on my pencil for a few minutes and then wrote:

> *The theme of this film was making friends. There was one boy the film said no one should have as a friend. He wore glasses and read books and had suspicious loner tendencies. We are supposed to watch out for people who are different like that. We should want to be like every-*

one else and then everyone will like us and want to be
friends. One girl in the film pulled up her socks and
tucked her blouse in. Other kids liked her then.

My conclusion from this film is that it is important to
have good grooming and to be punctual if you want to
have a lot of friends. Also to have blond hair and good
penmanship. Good penmanship helps you fit in.

I didn't even have to be ironic. That is exactly what the
film said.

We read our reports aloud. After I finished mine, Sister
said, "Yes, Francine, a good explanation of the dangers of
nonconformity." She wasn't being ironic, either.

The Perfect and Admirable Mary Agnes Malone raised
her hand, stood up, and said, "My father says the nail that
sticks up must be hammered back into place."

Sister nodded.

Sophie read hers in a loud voice. She said the film was
an attack on liberals and communists and other people the
government didn't like. She had to stand in the wastebasket
during recess.

Later, at lunch, we played Red Rover. Mary Virginia
called, "Red rover, red rover, let Sophie come over," and
Sophie came over.

Then Florence called, "Red rover, red rover, let Sophie
come over." Sophie ran back.

And Margie shouted, "*Red* rover, *red* rover, let Sophie
come over." Sophie went but much more slowly than before.

Gert yelled, "*Red* rover, *red* rover, let Sophie *commie*

over," and then all the girls screamed, "*Red* rover, *red* rover, let Sophie *commie* over!" Sophie walked away.

I stood there watching her go. Mary Virginia tapped me on the shoulder. "Come on, let's play Foursquare."

"But Sophie—"

"You already spend too much time with that weirdie," Mary Virginia said. "Remember what the film said about fitting in and making friends. Come on."

I followed Mary Virginia to where the other girls were gathered. They were already annoyed with me. I'd told them I couldn't have the slumber party because relatives were coming to stay all through the vacation, but I think they suspected it was because of Sophie. If I chose Sophie over them again, they would pick on me the way they picked on her.

Acrophobia means being afraid of heights. And people who are afraid of closed spaces have claustrophobia. Me, I have trouble-phobia, and it sometimes gets in the way of my doing what I want. Like now. I *did* want to speak up for Sophie. I *did* want to stand up for her, to take her side, to walk away with her. I really did.

But I didn't.

I always lost at Foursquare. But that day I played worse than usual because I was thinking about Sophie. The girls shouldn't have called her names, and I shouldn't have let her walk away alone. Abbott would never have let Costello go alone. Or Laurel desert Hardy. And there were always Three Stooges, not two. But I let Sophie walk away. Why, if I had been one of the Forty Martyrs of Sebaste who faced the Soldiers of the Thundering Legion, there'd be only Thirty-

Nine Martyrs. I would have gone and played Foursquare.

Sophie and I left school together as usual. "I hate this dumb school and dumb Sister Basil the Rotten and those dumb girls," she said on the way home. "Why can't they leave me alone?"

I was relieved that Sophie was blaming them and not mad at me for abandoning her. "They would leave you alone if you behaved better," I said.

"Maybe. Still, I get sick of being punished for being me."

"But you ask for it. You know you do."

"I'm just telling the truth and standing up for my rights and fighting injustice and—"

"Causing trouble for the fun of it."

She didn't say anything right away. Then she smiled. "I do liven things up, don't I?"

I cleared my throat. "I'm sorry," I said, "that I didn't stick up for you during Red Rover."

"Never mind. It was just a dumb game."

"I know, but I should have spoken up or walked away with you or something. I just couldn't. I'm not very brave."

"No, you're not. But you're braver than you used to be." I raised my eyebrows in inquiry. "You're my friend, aren't you, when no one else will be? That takes bravery."

"That's because being your friend hasn't caused me trouble yet. When it does, I don't know what I'll do. Isn't that an awful thing to admit?"

She socked me lightly on the arm as the bus bounced along. "'Feh, not to worry,' as Jacob Mandelbaum would say, 'until the sky hits you in the head.'"

Christmas vacation came, and Sophie and I had fun even without the slumber party. We found my old roller skates and, each wearing one skate, skated up and down Palm View Drive. We addressed Christmas cards for my mother, strung popcorn to hang on the tree, and wrote pretend letters to Santa Claus—I asked for a mink coat and Montgomery Clift. And I wrote a letter for Artie:

Dear Santa Claus,

I am writing this letter for my brother, Artie, who is five and a half and can't write yet. Artie can be a pain in the neck sometimes, like how he answers the phone "Duffy's Tavern" or spills Rice Krispies or sticks his lower lip out when he gets stubborn, but on the whole he is not a bad brother, so when he asked me to write to you, I said I would do it, even though I know there is no Santa Claus and my mother always buys the presents for him and wraps them herself, which anyone could tell as the paper is cut all crooked and the ribbons droop.

Artie says, "Please bring me a Hopalong Cassidy cowboy outfit and a Captain Midnight Decoder Ring, and I would rather get a new cap pistol than more underwear."

From Francine Green
private secretary to Mr. Arthur Green

On Christmas Eve we sang Christmas carols at the neighbors' doors even though it was hot enough to wear shorts, and the neighbors smiled at us over their martinis.

15

January 1950

Miss Velma Says I Could

I was lying on the rug in the living room, reading Betty Cavanna's *Going on Sixteen,* on loan from Susan Murphy, when someone walked in and stopped next to me. Wedge heels and ankle socks, hem of a flowered cotton housedress, scent of talcum powder. My mother.

"Are your thank-you notes finished?" she asked.

"I'm about to do them right now," I told her, and got up to get paper and pen.

"Hey, Francine," Artie called from his room, "want the tangerine from my Christmas stocking?"

"Why don't you want it?"

"Jocy Manila said if you swallow tangerine seeds, they start to grow into a tree in your stomach and the branches grow into your throat and choke you to death."

"Oh, Artie, that's not true."

"Joey Manila *said.*"

"Well," I said, "I myself think tangerine seeds in your

91

stomach might grow into tangerines, but it's too dark in there for leaves and branches, so no tree will grow and choke you. You'll simply be full of juicy fruit all the time. Just be careful not to eat too many, or you won't have room for cake."

"But Joey Manila *said.*"

"Joey Manila is a creep."

Artie sounded relieved. "Okay. I'll eat one seed from each tangerine."

"That ought to be just about right," I said.

I sat down at the kitchen table. I used to hate to write thank-you notes, especially for presents I wasn't truly thankful for, but since I discovered irony, I was finding the task much more pleasant. I spread my flowered notepaper on the table, filled my favorite pen with Schaefer's peacock blue ink, swung my hand back and forth over the paper a few times, and began to write:

Dear Aunt Martha and Uncle George,

Imagine my pleasure when I opened my presents Christmas morning, when it was 82 degrees here in Los Angeles, to find the plaid mittens-and-scarf set you sent me. What would I have done without it?

Yours truly,

Your niece,

Francine Green

P.S. Mother says she would call you on the phone if long distance weren't so expensive and I am to tell you hello for her. Hello.

I put it in a matching envelope, licked the flap, addressed it, and put it aside to await a stamp. One down.

My aunt Ellen had sent me *The Early Women Martyrs Coloring Book* and bunny pajamas. Ye gods. I picked up another sheet of paper.

"Francine," called my mother from the service porch, "I need you to go to the store and get milk, Crisco, and soap flakes. And apples if they're less than ten cents a pound."

"I'm doing my thank-you notes. Couldn't someone else go?"

She came to my side so abruptly that her starched apron crackled. "Do you *see* someone else? Is there someone else in this house I could send?"

My father was at work, Dolores out with Wally, and Artie too little. "No," I said.

"Should *I* go? Between changing the beds and doing the laundry and making dinner, do you want me to walk to the store for milk, Crisco, and soap flakes?"

"Okay, okay." I stacked the notepaper and capped the pen.

"Take a dollar from my dresser," my mother said, "and be sure to bring me the change. No Cokes or Popsicles."

I went into my parents' bedroom. It smelled like my mother—Cashmere Bouquet talcum powder and freshly ironed clothes. I sniffed all around but couldn't detect my father's martini-cigarette-shaving-cream smell. I sniffed through the hall and back into the living room, and pressed my nose into the back of his big chair. There it was.

Most men I knew smelled like martinis, cigarettes, and

shaving cream. Sometimes I wondered—if Jesus were alive today, would He smell like that, too? He'd have to get a haircut, that was for sure.

"Francine!" my mother shouted.

"I'm going, I'm going." And I did.

Why was it always me who had to watch Artie, write thank-you notes, go to the store? Always me. I felt like Mildred Pierce from the movie of that name, doing everything for someone who didn't appreciate it. Of course, Mildred was actually the mother and she did everything for her daughter, Veda, who not only didn't appreciate it but turned out to be a criminal and a murderer.

The January day was sunny and clear. The Ballantyne boys were working on their car as I passed. Skinny Mickey Sheen was washing the windows of his mother's house. And I could tell from the sweet odor of cut grass that Sally Rose around the corner was mowing her lawn again. I turned onto Pico and passed the laundromat, The Olde Smoke Shop, Kirby's Shoes, and Meeker's Radio Repair.

Miss Velma's Tap and Song Academy, Thorough Preparation for the Stage, had a poster in the window. I crossed the street to read it:

Be an actor! You can. Yes, you. Overcome shyness, stage fright, and speech impediments with Miss Velma's proven techniques. Miss Velma's students have gone on to be stars of stage, screen, and radio. You can too.

Me? Be an actress? I felt a flutter in my stomach. I could

be a movie star and go to premieres with Montgomery Clift. Thousands of cheering fans would admire and envy and imitate me. Me, the glamorous Francine Green, who always knew what to say. Miss Velma said I could.

I sang "The Surrey with the Fringe on Top" all the way to Petrov's Groceries. The junior class at No Sinners high school was going to perform *Oklahoma!* in the spring. Sister Saint Elmo had rewritten the play to leave out the Ado Annie character, because the nuns thought she was wild and a bad influence. Sophie would probably call it censorship and organize a rally.

The windows at Petrov's were covered with plywood, making the inside even darker than usual. "Gangsters break the windows and we have not the money to have them fixed again and again," Mrs. Petrov told me as she handed me the bag of milk, Crisco, and soap flakes. The apples were too expensive and had wrinkly skin. "And why they break them? Because we come from Russia and must be communists." She shook her head. "We leave Russia to escape the communists. Is funny, no?"

Walking home from the store was a lot harder than walking there. January or not, the hot California sun sat on my head like a blanket. I thought about what had happened to the Petrovs. It wasn't funny. It was scary. The war was over, and we won. Shouldn't we have peace now? Would we ever be safe? It was just not fair.

I sang "Life Is Just a Bowl of Cherries" all the way home. I was being ironic again. It was all I could think of to do.

16

Mr. Bowman Knows Irony

January turned cold and rainy. While Sophie and I made spaghetti and meatballs for dinner, Mr. Bowman chopped up lettuce for salad. He sang while he chopped. "Puccini," he said. "An Italian composer for our Italian dinner."

"*Mamma mia,*" said Sophie.

I put on my best Sister Basil the Rotten face and said, "The correct term, Miss Bowman, would be 'papa mia.'" Sophie nudged me and got spaghetti sauce on the white blouse of my uniform.

After dinner we sat by the big radio in their living room, listening to President Truman. He said he had ordered American scientists to begin development of a hydrogen bomb, a super bomb that would be a thousand times more powerful than the bombs we dropped on Japan at the end of the war.

It was like a horse kicked me in the stomach. My heart jumped and my mouth got dry. Super bombs? Plain old atomic bombs killed people and destroyed everything. What would *super* bombs do?

"Wonderful," said Mr. Bowman. "We will have the ability to kill everyone in the world a thousand times over. What an achievement! What a boon to mankind!" Holy cow, I thought, Mr. Bowman knows irony! "Super bombs. Have we gone crazy?"

We sat silent after President Truman finished. Finally Sophie cleared her throat. "I think Truman is a war criminal," she said. "I'm going to start a Ban the Bomb Club, with signs and banners. Maybe sweaters with *Ban the Bomb* embroidered on them." She stood up. "Come on, Francine. We can make plans while we do the dishes."

"No, stay, Francine. Sophie can do the dishes, and we'll talk," Mr. Bowman said. He got up, poured himself a cup of coffee from the pot on the dining table, and sat down again. "So what do you think about the bomb issue?"

He was asking *me?* He wanted *my* opinion? I thought a moment. "Well," I said finally, "Sister Rott . . . uh . . . Basil said bombs are forces for good because they could mean the end of godless communism."

"Bombs like this H-bomb could mean the end of everything. Every living thing. Did you know that? Some people are building bomb shelters in their backyards, but I think even if one could survive, one wouldn't want to live in the world that was left." He sipped his coffee noisily. "What do you think? Not Sister Basil. You."

Me? I looked quickly around to make sure Sister wasn't standing there, smiling, but I said nothing.

"Now that Russia has the bomb," he went on, "should

we develop a bigger one? And what if Russia develops an even bigger one? A K-bomb or a U-bomb or a Z-bomb? What should we do then?" He took another noisy sip of his coffee. "Speak up, Francine."

Speak up? What a notion, coming as I did from the land of "Sit down, Francine" and "Be quiet, Francine." What did I think? "I don't know," I told him.

"It's important to know what you think, my dear, or else you will be so hemmed in by other people's ideas and opinions, you won't have room for your own."

It was drizzling as I walked home. I remembered how, during the war, my family would gather around our big radio in the living room to listen to President Roosevelt. I'd sit on my father's lap, and although I didn't understand anything that was said, the president's familiar voice and my father's big arms made me feel safe and protected, even with a war on. Now Mr. Truman was president and there was talk about a hydrogen super bomb. Would we all die? Would *I* die? It was hard to imagine. I had a lump in my stomach, and it wasn't just from Sophie's meatballs.

Getting ready for bed that night, I sat at Dolores's dressing table and studied my worried face in the mirror. I tried so hard to be invisible, sometimes I felt like I wasn't here at all, like if I looked in the mirror, I would see no one there. What if someday there really *was* no Francine there, her having been smashed to bits by a super bomb?

Mr. Bowman thought I should speak up. If I were acting in a movie, I'd know what to say. I'd call President Truman and say—

No, even better, I'd send a telegram. People in movies always sent telegrams. A boy in a brown Western Union uniform bicycled up to someone's door and handed over an envelope. Women ripped them open and fainted dead away. Men would crumple them up and punch the wall. And soldiers sent telegrams to their girls that said: DARLING STOP I LEAVE IMMEDIATELY FOR THE FRONT STOP I MUST SEE YOUR FACE ONE LAST TIME STOP MEET ME UNDER THE CLOCK AT GRAND CENTRAL STATION AT NOON STOP LOVE STOP ELMER

I could see President Truman in his little glasses and bow tie opening the envelope and reading my telegram: DEAR MR PRESIDENT STOP I HEARD YOU ON THE RADIO TONIGHT TALKING ABOUT THE FUTURE STOP IF YOU ARE GOING TO TALK ABOUT THE FUTURE I THINK YOU SHOULD LET US HAVE ONE AND NOT BLOW US ALL UP STOP EVEN TO STOP COMMUNISTS STOP I AM AFRAID OF COMMUNISTS BUT I THINK I AM MORE AFRAID OF THE BOMB STOP I AM NOT SURE BUT I AM TRYING TO HAVE AN OPINION STOP YOURS TRULY STOP A CITIZEN

That would be much too long and expensive, and I didn't know how to send a telegram anyway, and in the *third* place I would be too nervous to actually send it.

Then I had a brainstorm. I picked up a pen. *Dear Montgomery Clift,* I wrote.

I am a girl with some troublesome questions and problems. The way you stood up to John Wayne in Red River *and fought for what you thought was right, although you were much younger and much smaller and had a lot to lose, made me think that you were a person who would*

understand and help me sort things out. I am worried about so much—my friend Sophie Bowman and the bomb and communists. People are telling me so many different things, and I don't know what to believe. Ordinarily I would talk to my friend Sophie about my problems, but as she is one of my problems right now, could I talk to you? You could call me at Olympic 3479, collect if necessary. I will figure out how to explain it to my parents. Or send me a letter at 1374 Palm View Drive. Thank you.

> *Your true eternal fan,*
> *Francine Green*

In *Photoplay* there was an address listed where you could send fan mail. I addressed and stamped the letter and left the house quietly in the dark to mail it before I lost what little nerve I had. My heart pounded like a Gene Krupa drum solo. This was not just my imagining. I was writing to a real person who would write back. And that real person was a movie star. And that movie star was Montgomery Clift!

The air was fresh and clean after the rain. The stars looked close enough for me to grab and put in my pocket.

My hand trembled as I dropped the letter into the mailbox. I held my breath, as if I expected J. Edgar Hoover and the FBI to come sweeping around the corner onto Palm View Drive and lock me up right there. All was quiet. I let out my breath and walked slowly home.

I climbed into bed and listened to Dolores's breathing

from the other bed, but I couldn't sleep. I had too many questions and no answers.

An airplane flew overhead. I held my breath until it was gone. Bombs. Ye gods. I pulled the pillow over my head and tried to think instead about Montgomery Clift reading my letter.

Nothing came of Sophie's Ban the Bomb Club. Sister Basil ripped down her posters, saying, "Shame on you, Miss Bowman, bringing communist ideas into our school." And no one wanted to join, not even me.

Some days later Sophie came over for supper. Dolores was out with Wally, and Artie was in bed with a cold, so only the four of us were there for

DINNER AT THE GREENS', The Sophie Episode

MOTHER: Come on, you two. You can set the table.

SOPHIE: Right away, Mrs. Green.

FRANCINE: What are we having?

MOTHER: Macaroni and cheese, corn, and yellow cake. I know how you like yellow cake.

FRANCINE: Yikes, an all-yellow meal. See, Sophie, I told you she liked things to match.

MOTHER: If you have complaints about supper, young lady, you may skip it and go right to bed.

FRANCINE: Sorry.

MOTHER: Fred, Sophie is here for supper.

FATHER *(with a mouth full of corn)*: Hrghhll.

MOTHER *(passing the macaroni)*: Here, Sophie dear.

FRANCINE *(silently)*: "Sophie dear"? The only time I hear "dear" around here is when we're talking about Bambi.

SOPHIE: This is delicious, Mrs. Green. How ever did you make it so tasty?

MOTHER: I have a secret ingredient. I put a dash of A1 Steak Sauce in it.

SOPHIE: Well, it's just delicious.

FRANCINE *(silently)*: Oh nausea.

MOTHER: Francine, you clear the table and start the dishes. I want to show Sophie some of my recipes.

FRANCINE: But I did the dishes last—

FATHER *(ruffling Francine's hair)*: That's enough, Francine Louise. Just do what your mother says.

After dinner I walked Sophie halfway home. Neither of us said anything for a long time. Finally I said, "How come all of a sudden you care more about macaroni and meatloaf than free speech and such?"

"What do you mean?" she asked.

"You and my mother sure were buddy-buddy over those recipes."

"Are you jealous, Francine Louise?"

"Jealous? Me? Don't be silly." Of course I wasn't jealous. It was only my ordinary, boring, annoying mother.

"Well, good. Your mother was just being nice to me."

"It's more than that, Sophie. She never tells *anybody* about the steak sauce in the macaroni."

"I enjoyed having a family for an evening," Sophie said.

"Your father is pretty great. Isn't he enough family for you?"

"Family? Harry is more like a teacher or something. He likes to make speeches and educate me, but he's not exactly father material."

"Oh, Sophie, how can you say that? He's the best father ever. He lets you call him Harry. He never says 'That's enough, Sophie' or 'Sit down and be quiet, Sophie,' and he never gets mad when you get into trouble for doing stupid things."

"Fathers should make you feel safe," she said. "I never feel safe."

I thought about that as I walked home. My father was sitting on our porch when I got there. I could see the tip of his cigarette glowing in the darkness. "I was just making sure you got home all right," he said, and put his arm across my shoulders as we went in.

17

February 1950

Francine and Sophie Talk About Life

"Mother, can I go to the movies with Sophie next Saturday?"

"We're playing canasta with the Willbanks on Saturday," she said. "Dolores will be out with Wally, and we'll need someone to watch Arthur."

"I'll be home by eight," I told her.

"What movie? Are you sure it's nothing we'd object to?"

"It's a musical. Mr. Bowman's friend, Jacob Mandelbaum, has a part in it. Imagine, just imagine, going to a Hollywood premiere and knowing someone who is in the movie!"

"I don't have to imagine. I'm sure you'll be telling me about it for days. You may go, as long as you're home by eight."

I went to the Bowmans's. The Sunday afternoon was rainy, long, and lazy. We were happy to stay inside and do little. "It's not a Hollywood premiere, you know, Francine," she said, pushing me in the rocker with her foot. "It's one of his old pictures. It's a benefit."

"What's a benefit?"

"It's something to raise money for somebody. This one is for Mr. Mandelbaum."

"I thought he was a movie actor. Why does he need money?"

"He's been blacklisted."

"What's blacklisted?"

"Jeeps, Francine. Where have you been? Blacklisted means he's on a list of people supposedly suspicious or subversive, and no one will hire him anymore."

I put my feet down, and the rocking stopped abruptly. "You mean he's a communist? I thought he was a real Yankee Doodle."

"You don't have to be a communist to be blacklisted. Lots of ordinary people have been blacklisted. You know, like the Hollywood Ten."

"What's the Hollywood Ten? Sounds like a baseball team."

"You dope," Sophie said, laughing. "It's been in the newspaper for years. They're screenwriters from Hollywood who the government wants to put in jail for refusing to answer questions about maybe being communists. I mean, some guy asks them questions that are none of his business, and when they say, 'It's none of your business,' bingo, they're criminals, and they can't work because no studio will hire them. That's blacklisting."

"But if they weren't communists, why wouldn't they just say so?"

"It's a matter of free speech. People have the right to speak and the right not to speak."

"And if they *are* communists, shouldn't they go to jail?"

"Being a communist is not a crime in this country, Francine," said Mr. Bowman, coming in the front door and shaking water off like a wet dog. "Not yet anyway." He took off his hat and brushed his hair back.

At the door of his study he turned and said, "This anti-communist madness, like all madness, will get out of control. Mark my words. Yesterday I heard that a butcher on Melrose was picketed for advertising Polish hams." He gave a barklike little laugh, but I wasn't sure whether it was a joke or not.

Why wasn't being a communist a crime? Except for Sophie and Mr. Mandelbaum and maybe Mr. Bowman, people seemed to think communists were dangerous and un-American, that they would use any means, even the movies, to betray and destroy us. We had to be vigilant. "This movie we're seeing on Saturday isn't about communists, is it?" I asked Sophie, being vigilant. "You said it was a musical."

"It's about a boy and girl trying to win a dance contest. His father is a dentist."

"That should be okay, then." I didn't think there were communist dentists, but still I was anxious. Sister once said that most movie people were communists. I hoped there wouldn't be communists at the benefit, kidnapping people and shipping them to Russia or East Germany.

"What kind of movies does your father write?" I asked Sophie, worried that she'd say communist propaganda films about the glories of Russia.

"He's a serious drama kind of guy."

"Like what? I've never seen 'Written by Mr. Harry Bowman' up on the screen."

"That's because there's no movie yet with his name on it. He says he writes a script, someone is brought in to rewrite, someone else to mutilate, and someone else to destroy. And the destroyer gets the screen credit."

That couldn't be true. I was certain that movie people were as wonderful as the movies. Maybe Mr. Bowman just wasn't a very good writer yet. "What if he wrote a movie for Montgomery Clift someday? Wouldn't that be too much?" I rocked quietly for a minute, relishing the thought. "What about you?" I asked her finally. "Do you think you'll be a writer, too?"

"You bet. I'm going to be a crusading reporter and expose injustice wherever I find it." She leaned over and picked up the shiny wooden nut bowl from the coffee table. After examining all the nuts carefully, she selected one. "I'll never get married—no husband, no kids. Just dogs. And a green convertible." The nutcracker closed on the nut with a sharp sound. "What about you?"

Be an actor, Miss Velma had said, but I wasn't ready to tell anyone about that yet, not even Sophie. "Probably I'll just live with my parents all my life," I told her. "Maybe they'll let me get a cat or a parakeet or something." I thought about it while Sophie continued demolishing nuts. Catholic girls who didn't become nuns were supposed to be Catholic wives and mothers. I didn't want to be a nun, but I couldn't imagine getting married. I still hadn't spoken a word to Gordon, much less had a date. I'd have to get a job somewhere.

My father worked for a company on Wilshire Boulevard that built housing developments in the San Fernando Valley. He was a member of the International Federation of Professional and Technical Engineers, and his union dues were the only bill he ever paid without grumbling. My mother did the laundry, made martoonies, and cut out coupons to save money. For fun they played canasta and listened to *Fibber McGee and Molly* on the radio. I didn't want to be like them.

The question of my future had been on my mind ever since Vocation Day, when our class was visited by student nuns from the Order of Mary Help of Sinners, to which our Sisters belonged. They visited eighth-grade classes all over Los Angeles every year to share with us the joys of nunhood, joys so great we would want to be like them—living together all their lives, never getting married or having babies, singing and praying and working in eternal poverty, chastity, and obedience.

The student nuns were young and perky, not at all the type I would imagine wanting to be nuns. They wore short skirts and tiny white veils that left their hair mostly uncovered. One called Miss O'Hara giggled a lot and had wavy red hair that fell to her waist. I couldn't imagine why she'd want to hide in a convent all her life.

After the visitors left, Sister Basil had asked us, "How many of you girls aspire to join the Holy Sisterhood?"

The Perfect and Admirable Mary Agnes Malone was the first to raise her hand, of course, and then most of the girls raised theirs, too. Susan, Gert, Sophie, and I were the only ones with our hands still folded on our desks. Sister stared at Susan until her hand went up, and then Gert's followed. It was just Sophie and me. Unlike most Catholic girls, I'd never wanted to be a nun. I thought about being a saint sometimes—it seemed the highest calling to which a Catholic girl could aspire, since Mother of God was already taken—but never a nun.

Sister walked a little way down the aisle and stood next to my desk, looking right at me, her black eyebrows like a slash across her white face. When she raised her left eyebrow, I could feel my hand begin to rise, as if a string were tied from that eyebrow to my arm. Slowly, slowly, up it went. And Sister nodded.

She looked at Sophie for a minute but shrugged and walked away. Even Sister Basil could only do so much.

A note was waggled at me. *A nun? You don't really want to, do you?*

Jeepers, no. I didn't want to raise my hand, but it was like I couldn't help it. I think Sister Rotten has magical powers.

Could you believe the part about poverty, chastity, and obedience?

No money, no men, and no mind of your own. Sounds a lot like my life.

Suddenly Sister was standing beside me, so close I could smell the slightly sweet and soapy nun smell of her. She was swinging her rosary beads and smiling. "Francine, would you care to share with the class what you find so interesting?"

My heart jumped and a shiver ran through my body. Sophie stood up, pocketing the note. "It was not Francine but me, Sister," she said. "I was being rude, impertinent, and blasphemous, as usual. Do you want me to go stand in the trash can?"

"Sit down," Sister growled.

Since that day a week ago I had been wondering about my future. And now Sophie had asked, "What about you?" Well, what about me? Could I really be an actress? I imagined myself on a movie set with Montgomery Clift or Clark Gable, starring in some romantic drama, tingling with excitement, opening my mou— . . . That's as far as I got. Even in my daydream I couldn't open my mouth. It would take some sort of miracle to turn *me* into a movie star.

"I suppose I could work in a pet store," I told Sophie, "feed the hamsters or something." Yes, that sounded more like me.

The afternoon drifted away. And the whole week. Still no letter from Monty. On Saturday we went to the movie. Mr. Mandelbaum played a friendly shopkeeper named Mr. Smiley. He still seemed like Mr. Mandelbaum, only in a white apron. I don't know if I'd call that *acting*.

I was nervous, but no communists tried to kidnap me. It was just a movie.

18

Mr. Roberts

It was raining again as I walked Sophie home after school. "Want to stay for dinner?" she asked.

"I don't know," I said. "I have to find a book for my book report."

"My dad has a million books in his den. You can borrow one of them."

We went into a small room lined with bookcases to the ceiling. Photographs of Franklin Roosevelt, Jackie Robinson, and a woman who looked a lot like Sophie stood on the desk.

"Here," Sophie said, grabbing a book off the seat of a soft leather chair. "Try this."

"Are you crazy?" I said, examining the book jacket. "I can't do a report on a book named *The Naked and the Dead*. Sister would hang me by my ears in the playground."

Sophie laughed and poked me with her elbow. "I know, dummy. I was joking."

"A joke? Really? It's about time," I said.

She pulled another book from the shelves. "How about this one? My father actually laughed."

There was a soldier or sailor or somebody on the cover. "I don't like war books."

She held the book above her head. "Well, perhaps that's for the best," she said. "There's no guns or fighting in this, but from what I hear, it's not exactly for children. Maybe it's too old for y—"

I grabbed it. *Mr. Roberts*. It had to be better than *Dotty Dimple Out West*. I looked around the room. "So many books," I said. The books we owned wouldn't have filled half a shelf. "Did your father write any of them?" I asked Sophie.

"No, he mostly just writes his movie scripts, which mostly don't get made into movies, even when the studio assigns him one to write, which they aren't doing right now."

"Why not?"

"He thinks it's because he helped with the benefit for Jacob Mandelbaum. His agent told him he's suspected of having 'communist sympathies.'"

Jeepers. Was that true? I looked quickly around the room, afraid I'd see a hammer and sickle magically appear on the wall. "Does he?"

"Have communist sympathies? You mean, like trying to help a friend who can't work because of his beliefs? Belonging to the Screenwriters' Guild and the Committee for the First Amendment? If you call that having communist sympathies, then yes, I guess he does." She sat down, and her shoulders slumped. She pushed her hair back in that way she did. "I'm worried about him. What if he can't work? Or gets put in jail? What would I *do?*"

I couldn't imagine Mr. Bowman in jail. I couldn't imagine any of it—A-bombs and H-bombs, communist sympathies, losing your job or worse. It was like something out of a horror movie. "You could always live with us, Sophie." I said, "but probably it won't come to that. Maybe you could talk to your father and ask him to be more careful. Not speak up so much or call attention to himself. Not get involved. Maybe he should—"

"Give it a rest, Francine," she said. "What do you know about it?" Her words were clipped and sharp edged, as if she had cut them with a knife.

I was startled and a little bit hurt. If free speech meant Mr. Bowman saying what he really thought, then free speech meant I could say what I thought. But Sophie didn't seem to see it that way.

All the talk about communists made my stomach hurt. I didn't feel like staying for dinner. I told Sophie I had to go home, even though it was my mother's meatless Wednesday—spaghetti and rice balls. You'd think there was still a war on.

Sophie walked me toward the front door. Mr. Bowman was sitting on the couch with a martini, listening to the radio. He didn't even notice us. "Today," the voice on the radio was saying, "Senator Joseph McCarthy of Wisconsin claimed he had a list of 205 people working in our government who are known to be members of the Communist Party."

Mr. Bowman grunted and took a sip of his martini. When the newscast paused for a commercial—"Lucky Strike means fine tobacco"—I sat down on the arm of the couch. "Is that true?" I asked Mr. Bowman. "Are there really communists in the government?"

"I don't know, Francine," he said, "and neither does Senator McCarthy or anyone else. And what if there are? Is there any proof that they are disloyal or dangerous or planning to overthrow the government? Innocent people will suffer, mark my words."

I stomped in puddles all the way home. I was not happy (splash!). I wanted the world to be clean and neat, black and white. I wanted the bad guys to be punished, the good rewarded, and I wanted it to be easy to tell who was who (splash!). I wanted the government to be right and fair, to keep us safe and out of war. I wanted communists to go back to Russia and get rid of their bombs. I wanted Americans to get rid of *our* bombs (splash!). I wanted the world to be like I thought it was when I was four or five. It was much too scary now that I was thirteen (splash! *splash!*).

To take my mind off communists and bombs, I started reading *Mr. Roberts* when I got home. I kept reading, even through the boring parts. I wanted to see what had made Mr. Bowman laugh.

Mr. Roberts is the story of the men aboard a supply ship in the South Pacific in World War Two. They didn't fight but took food and toothpaste and toilet paper to those who did. The captain of the ship was mean and nasty, and all the men hated him. They called him Stupid behind his back. Stupid grew palm trees in buckets by the door of his cabin. They were the joy of his life. Mr. Roberts was the first lieutenant. The men loved him because he stood up for them when they got in trouble from the captain's stupid rules like no chewing gum or no taking off your shirt when it is hot. Once when the captain was especially mean to some poor sailor, Mr. Roberts threw the palm trees overboard. The crew made him a medal.

"I'm reading *Mr. Roberts*," I told Sophie later, "but I can't write a book report about it."

"Why not?" she asked.

"Are you kidding? Sister would never approve. It's all about sailors drinking, using bad language, and chasing women."

"So what? Probably that's what sailors do."

I shook my head. "Doesn't matter. Sister would never approve. How come your father read this, anyway? I thought he only read serious books that improve your mind."

"Someone gave it to him. She thought it might make a good movie."

"I guess it would if they left out all the boring parts."

I didn't have time to read another book, so I wrote a report on *A Tree Grows in Brooklyn* again. I got a B+. At No Sinners, being approved is more important than being original.

19

March 1950

Oklahoma! and Lepers and Mary's Maidens

When I got home from school, I checked the mail. Still nothing from Montgomery Clift.

Dolores called from our bedroom, "Francine, is that you?" She grabbed me as I walked in. "I need your help."

Me? Dolores was asking me for help? I was overcome and speechless.

"You know the high school is doing *Oklahoma!*?"

I nodded.

"Well, I'm going to try out."

"But Dolores, you can't sing a note."

"I'm sure there'll be some non-singing parts."

"How could there be—it's a musical."

Dolores socked me in the arm. "Stop interrupting. As I said, long ago, before you started pestering me about singing, I want to try out. I have to prepare a scene for my audition. Will you help me?"

"You mean like act with you, in front of people?" My

legs turned to jelly at the very thought. Obviously I wasn't ready to be a movie star yet. "I couldn't, I just couldn't."

"You don't have to audition, you drip, just help me find a scene to do and rehearse it with me."

"What kind of scene?"

"I don't know. Doesn't one of those books you're always reading have a scene I could act out?"

I thought for a moment. "I have a great idea. We just saw a movie about Father Damien in class. You know, the priest who went to Hawaii to work with lepers whose noses and ears were falling off and stuff." Dolores grimaced. "Just listen. Every day he preached to them, beginning, 'My friends.' One day he was soaking his feet in a bucket of boiling water and he could not feel the heat, and he knew that meant he had caught leprosy. So the next morning he stood up to give his sermon, and he said, 'My fellow lepers,' and everyone knew that he had leprosy too. Isn't that the end? It breaks me up every time. You could do that scene for your audition. 'My fellow lepers.' It just kills me."

"That's one line, Francine. I have to prepare more than one line."

"But—"

"No. Nothing about lepers. What else you got?"

"I read a play about George Washington in the—"

"Will you be serious? I need something romantic or dramatic."

"How about Beth's death scene from *Little Women*? It's dramatic."

"I never read it."

"Honestly, Dolores, you might as well be illiterate. I know you saw the movie. Remember? Elizabeth Taylor and Margaret O'Brien and Peter Lawford?" We both sighed, thinking of Peter Lawford.

"Well, maybe if I could play the Elizabeth Taylor part," Dolores said, fluffing her hair.

"Elizabeth Taylor wasn't in that scene. You should be Beth. It could go something like this."

I instructed Dolores to lie down on her bed and put a hairbrush in her hands like a flower. "'Oh sorrow,' I say. I'm Jo. 'Oh sorrow, our blessed saintly Beth is leaving us. She is so kind and good and always tried to do right. What will we do without her?' And Jo looks out the window where spring is approaching in their little garden, kind of sniffles a little, and says, 'The birds and the flowers have come to say good-bye to our Beth and I must be brave. I love you, my Beth. Sleep well.' Now, Dolores, you cough sort of delicately and breathe a big breath like a sigh and die."

"Francine, Jo has all the lines."

"Well, then, you could be Jo."

Dolores shook her head. "I'm not going to play some tomboy with a man's name."

"I'm trying to help you, Dolores, but you just won't be helped. Why don't you read some lines from the script of *Oklahoma!*?"

"Boring. Everyone will be doing that. I wanted to do something more interesting, some part that has lines and where I don't have to be called Jo. Can't you find anything good?"

I thought Dolores shouldn't be so snippy to someone she had asked for a favor. I had half a mind to tell her to find something herself. But this challenge was right up my alley. I knew I could come up with the perfect romantic and dramatic scene, even if I had to write it myself.

At school the next day, Sister had a surprise for us. "This Friday," she said, "there will be a prayer meeting at Gilmore Field sponsored by Mary's Maidens. Mrs. Thomas Murray, one of the organizers of the event, will be here today to tell us about Mary's Maidens, and I would like to make a bargain with you. If you behave, all of you," she said, looking straight at Sophie, "behave, and do not shame me in front of Mrs. Murray, we will attend the prayer meeting."

We all cheered, in a subdued, Catholic-school sort of way. Getting out of the Sin-Free Institute for Truly Feminine People was a rare treat.

Mrs. Thomas Murray came in after lunch. She was old, but in a strong sort of way, with kind blue eyes and silver hair piled high on her head. She was dressed all in blue, as befitted a Mary's Maiden, I thought, and spoke in a soft voice that made you want to listen. If I had to get old someday, I thought I'd like to get old like that.

We all sat quietly, hands folded on our desks, as she began to speak. "We, Mary's Maidens, are women of all ages who seek to grow in holiness through prayer and service to others. We try to listen to God and His Holy Mother in the quiet of our hearts and do what they bid us, whether it be collecting and distributing food and clothing to the poor or sponsoring prayer meetings for the intentions of His holy church." She sounded a little like the Blessed Martin de Porres Sophie had spoken about at the speech contest. I was sure that Sophie would want to join right away.

"On Friday we will gather together with girls from Catholic schools throughout the Los Angeles area to ask God's Holy Mother to inspire our hearts to do as God commands, without pride or desire for acclaim, but humbly, as the early Christians did, brother and sister caring for one another." Her face shone with faith and commitment. Sister beamed at her. "Will you come? Will you join your prayers to ours?"

The Perfect and Admirable Mary Agnes Malone, of course, weasely Weslia, Florence, and some others stood and said, "We will, we will," but in the seat in front of me, Sophie stiffened. I could tell from her back that she was going to say something, something disruptive, and we would not be going to the prayer meeting.

She started to stand, but I pulled on her sweater. "No, Sophie, don't. Please don't."

Mrs. Murray said, "Do you young ladies have a question?" I knew when I was beaten. I let go of Sophie and she stood up. The other girls groaned.

"Mrs. Murray, from what Sister says, the early Christians were very much like communists, living and working together, holding all their goods in common, and distributing them to each according to his need. Do you mean we should pray to be communists?"

Mrs. Murray frowned. "My dear child, you—"

Sophie wasn't finished. "The way Sister described Jesus

and his apostles, I think they were communists, too, working together for the benefit of all, sharing their food and possessions, no man seeking to be greater or richer than another. Sister said they—"

Mrs. Murray turned toward Sister, her blue eyes sad and puzzled and horrified at the same time. "Sister, just what is it you are teaching these children?"

I stopped listening. It was over. We would not be going anywhere. I looked at Sister. She had tears in her eyes. Yes, Sister Basil the Rotten, with actual tears in her eyes. Who would have thought it?

Sister was so distressed that she neglected to make Sophie stay after school. Sophie and I left together, but I walked quickly ahead of her to the bus stop. "Francine, wait," she called, but I wouldn't. I sat in the back of the bus, far from our regular seats, but she followed me and sat down.

I looked at her. "Sophie, why? Why did you spoil it for everybody?"

"Oh, she was such a goody-goody, I just had to ruffle her up a bit. What's the problem? Did you really want to go to this prayer thing?"

"Actually, Mary's Maidens sounds kind of interesting. They do good work, and besides, we would have gotten out of school for a day. But that's not the point. Other people wanted to go and you ruined it."

"I have the right to speak up, to say what I want. Free speech—"

"I've heard all that before, Sophie Bowman. Your idea of

free speech is 'act like a two-year-old and make trouble.' I don't think that's what the Constitution means by free speech. Did you ever think about keeping your mouth shut sometimes?" I surprised myself, having the nerve to say that to Sophie, but just then I didn't care if I ever saw her and her big mouth again. I turned away and looked out the window.

We got off the bus in silence and walked toward home. Finally Sophie said, "I'm sorry, Francine, sorry I spoiled things for you. I guess I didn't have to tell her my communist apostle theory just then."

I could tell Sophie didn't understand, but I knew I would forgive her anyway.

20

Joan of Arc

The house was perfectly quiet and still smelled of our dinner meatloaf. My mother and father had gone to the movies to see Bette Davis in *All About Eve,* but I wasn't allowed to go with them because of Artie.

"Why can't Dolores be in charge of Artie?" I'd asked. "He's sleeping and won't be any trouble."

"Dolores has homework," my mother said.

"So do I."

"Well, then, that's another reason you can't go to the movies." She straightened her hat and pulled on her white gloves. "Dolores needs to concentrate and study very hard or she'll be in real danger of being a junior again next year. Let her work, and you take care of Artie and the dishes." She kissed me on the cheek, took my father's arm, and left.

I rubbed at the sweet, sticky mark her lipstick left on my cheek. Why did I have to do everything? I thought as I dried the dinner plates. And the "everything" was so boring. I wished something exciting would happen to me, like being asked to star in a movie with Montgomery Clift, or the Virgin Mary appearing and telling me holy secrets, or God calling me to lead soldiers to save France like Joan of—

I threw the dish towel into the air. Of course. Joan of Arc! It was a brilliant idea. It was dramatic and romantic, and the nuns would love it. Dolores could audition with a scene about Joan of Arc. All I had to do was write it.

The next day after dinner, I found Dolores at her dressing table, pinning to the mirror frame what was either a dried corsage of yellow roses or a cabbage. "I have just the audition scene for you, Dolores. Joan of Arc."

"Remind me who she is," she said.

"Dolores, you remember every shade of nail polish Revlon ever made and you can't remember who Joan of Arc is?"

"If you're going to be snotty, you can leave."

"Okay, okay. Just listen. Picture this. England has invaded France, and Charles, the rightful king of France, sits useless in a palace in Paris. One day Joan, a French peasant girl of fourteen, is laboring in her father's fields. Labor, Dolores. You're Joan."

Dolores stood and sort of waved her arms around.

"You look like you're dusting the dining room," I said. "Labor, Dolores! Dig or plow or something." She waved her arms around a bit more. "Okay, Joan is laboring in the field when a brilliant figure with wings and a flaming sword" (I brandished the toilet plunger I'd brought from the bathroom) "appears to her. I'll be Saint Michael and say 'Joan, you are to lead a mighty army and save France from the dreadful English.' Now, Dolores, you read this."

Dolores put on her glasses, took the script, and read, "'Why me, a peasant girl who can neither ride nor fight? Nor read nor write nor—'"

I took the script back. "'That matters not. I am Saint Michael, but it is God who commands you.' Now Saint Michael disappears, replaced by a beautiful girl with long golden hair with her foot on the head of a dragon. 'I am Saint Margaret, and I am here to tell you that Saint Michael is correct. God has chosen you to save France.' You read here, Dolores."

Dolores cleared her throat and said, "'I am but a weak woman, and I am a fright and—'"

"Not a fright, Dolores. Affrighted."

"What the heck does that mean?"

"It means frightened, scared."

"Then why can't I say that?"

"Affrighted is so much more poetic. But okay, say frightened."

Dolores cleared her throat again, and her voice rang out. "'I am but a weak woman, and I am frightened—'"

"Come on, Dolores, you've got to sound frightened. Like this." I hunched my shoulders and whispered, 'I am but a weak woman, and I am frightened and much too cowardly to lead an army.' And Saint Margaret says, 'Oh Joan, my dear, I too was but a weak woman, but when threatened with death for being a Christian, I found the strength to resist, even when swallowed by a dragon, which I caused to burst asunder and—'"

"Francine," said Dolores, pulling on my arm, "the saints have all the lines."

"No, wait." I turned the page. "Now you read this, where Joan says, 'What is it God commands me to do?' And Saint Margaret answers, 'Go to Charles in Paris and tell him that it is God's will that you put on armor and raise a mighty army to drive the English out of France and crown him king.' Joan paces around like this for a while" (I paced and wrung my hands) "for she is sore afraid and reluctant to ride a horse and lead a bunch of strangers to battle, but gradually she can feel her sense of duty outweigh her fears. And here, Dolores, you'd gradually stand straighter and taller, and then say—"

I looked for Dolores, but she wasn't there. "Dolores?"

"Hi, Wally, it's Dolores," she said into the telephone in the hall. "Hold on a minute." She called to me, "Never mind, Francine. I'm going to read a scene from *Oklahoma!*"

She did, and she was cast as Third Farmer's Wife. No lines, but it was a part, and she got her name in the program.

I put the script for Joan of Arc under the half slips in my underwear drawer. I might need it someday if I were to audition for something. After all, acting might run in the family.

21

Hooray for Hollywood!

After days and days of rain, Monday dawned sunny and mild. "I can't bear the thought of going to school on a day like this," said Sophie as we bounced along in the bus, past liquor stores and palm trees and little stucco houses in candy colors, motor courts and used-car lots and big gray buildings full of dentists. "Why don't we just stay on the bus until it gets somewhere interesting, somewhere we could have an adventure?"

"Yes, someplace like Chicago," I said. "Or New York. Or Hoboken."

"What's Hoboken?" she asked.

"A city in New Jersey. That's where Frankie Sinatra's from. He's swoony." I thought a minute. "Wouldn't it be neat if this bus could fly? We could be in Hoboken like that," I said, snapping my fingers. "Or in Europe. Spain, maybe, or Italy."

"Or Paris," Sophie said, "where we'll smoke skinny black cigarettes and write dark, tragic poems."

I took a deep drag on my #2 pencil. "We'll be pursued by handsome French painters, be madcap romantics, and have high jinks and tomfoolery. Hey," I said, knocking my knee against hers, "on Saturday let's go to Hollywood. We could have high jinks there. And maybe see movie stars."

"Let's go *today,* Francine. Look," she said, pointing to a billboard out the window. "It was meant to be."

The comedy team of Dean Martin and Jerry Lewis, proclaimed the billboard, onstage, in person, before the movie at the Egyptian Theater. In Hollywood. Today.

"Dean Martin is on the cover of the new *Look* magazine," Sophie said. "He's pretty dreamy. Let's go see him."

Me, I definitely preferred Jerry Lewis, with his rubber legs and funny faces. "Hey, lay-deee," he'd say, and I'd laugh until I snorted out my nose.

"Why don't we just stay on the bus, skip school, and see Martin and Lewis?" Sophie asked me.

"Okay."

She stared at me. "You mean it?"

"Sure. Let's just forget about school and fool around in Hollywood. Maybe we could skip school tomorrow, too, and go to Mexico or San Francisco. In fact, we could skip school forever and just travel the world having adventures."

"Really? Would you?"

I took a deep breath. "No, no, and no. Of course not. I was being ironic."

"I know *that,* silly. I meant today. Would you go today?"

"No. We'd get in trouble."

"Jeeps, Francine, don't be such a dishrag. Sister Basil the

Not-So-Great is away this week, remember, and Sister Saint Elmo never knows who's there and who isn't. No missing Sophie and Francine, no trouble. Come on. Let's go. We could have lunch in a drugstore. I have enough money for both of us."

I reached up to pull the cord to signal the driver. "I can't do it. I'd worry too much."

"Too late now," Sophie said. "We passed our stop long ago. If we go back, we'll just be late and have to stay after school. If we don't go at all, they'll probably just think we're out sick."

"The Perfect and Admirable Mary Agnes Malone won't."

"Who cares? Sister Saint Elmo pays no attention to her."

"That's because Sister Saint Elmo can't hear."

"So, no problem. Come on, Francine. Live a little." We were way past our stop by then. My palms were sweaty and my head ached. As I sat down again, I knew I would regret it.

We rode all the way to Hollywood, watching the houses and shops give way to department stores, nightclubs, and drive-in restaurants with carhops on roller skates. The rain had cleared the gray-and-yellow smog away. The hills were green, and I could see snow high on the mountains to the east.

The scared feeling in my stomach gradually gave way to curiosity and excitement. Hollywood. Jerry Lewis. Movie stars. I began to feel a bit like one of the sisters in *My Sister Eileen,* who had madcap adventures and high jinks in New York. Maybe handsome foreign sailors would fall in love with us and follow us through the streets like in the book. I patted my hair and sat up a little straighter.

At Highland we got off the bus, took off our beanies, and stuffed our blue All Saints sweaters into our book bags. We walked up Highland, past Selma, and there we were— Hollywood Boulevard. No movie stars, but grand theaters, used-book shops with dusty windows, and little coffee shops that smelled like bacon.

The Egyptian wasn't as famous as Grauman's Chinese down the street, but in the courtyard, guarded by sphinxes and a giant dog-headed god, I was Cleopatra, sailing down the Nile on a barge, loved by men and coddled by my slaves. "Peel me a grape," I'd command them. "Shade me with an umbrella lest I sunburn and freckle."

"Come on, stop dreaming," Sophie said, waving the tickets. "This cost me seventy cents, so I don't want to miss a minute."

Inside, the theater was nearly as big as the train station downtown. It was cool, white and gold except for the scarlet draperies, red plush seats, and a ceiling so blue you felt there was no end to it but Heaven itself. An usher in a shiny white uniform trimmed with gold braid tried to show us to seats downstairs, but it was too crowded. We shook our heads and went up into the first balcony, where we sat behind an empty row and put our feet up on the seats in front. When the red velvet curtains parted, there was a hush, as if we were in church and the pope himself was coming out to entertain us.

Dean Martin *was* dreamy, and Jerry Lewis just as funny

as in *My Friend Irma*. He walked on his ankles, and said, "Awww, Deeeeeeean," and pretended to lead the orchestra. We laughed and laughed.

The movie was a western with John Wayne. I'd had enough of cowboys, what with Artie and his new Hopalong Cassidy outfit, and Sophie was hungry, so we didn't stay.

We went to Walgreen's for tuna on wheat toast and cherry Cokes, but the tuna sandwich sat like a lump in my stomach. "We'd better go home now," I said, feeling a little uneasy.

"We can't. How could you show up in the middle of the afternoon? What would you tell your mom? We'll have to wait until after school." Sophie pulled on my arm. "Come on. Let's go listen to records. 'It's Music City, Sunset and Vine,'" she sang, like the commercial on the radio, and headed for the record store. I followed her but kept looking behind me for Sister Basil, as if she were not at a retreat for Catholic-school principals at all but had gone to see Martin and Lewis at the Egyptian and was now headed to Wallich's Music City, where she would catch up with us and—

"Come *on*," said Sophie, pulling me faster. And soon we were both singing, "It's Music City, Sunset and Vine," swinging our hands and running through the door of Music City.

"'You're Breaking My Heart,'" I said to a skinny clerk with watery eyes and a mustache.

"And we hardly know each other," he said with a wink.

My face flamed up. "No. I want to listen to 'You're Breaking My Heart,' by Vic Damone."

He pulled a record from the row behind the counter, put it into a green paper sleeve, and handed it to me. Sophie and I went into one of the little glass booths, put the record on the turntable, and listened to it over and over. It was so romantic. I closed my eyes and imagined Gordon Riley singing to me as I was leaving him for another and breaking his heart. No, even better, the Perfect and Admirable Mary Agnes Malone was singing as Gordon left *her* for *me,* his own true love. Yes, much better.

Finally the clerk knocked on the glass and frowned. I put the record back into the sleeve and handed it to him as we left. Twelve times! Vic Damone had sung to me twelve times!

As we headed home on the bus, the curiosity and excitement abandoned me entirely. "This doesn't seem like fun anymore," I said. "I can't believe I let you talk me into it. My parents will kill me."

"They won't even know."

"They know everything."

"Francine," my mother said as soon as we walked in, "where have you been? Sister Peter Claver called. You missed your shift at the library." She dried her hands, smoothed her apron, and looked at me.

Sister Pete. Jeepers, I had forgotten.

"Where were you?" she asked again, her eyes so sharp they could peel radishes.

"I . . . we . . . I . . ." I felt hot all over, and my stomach tumbled. I wished I could just say "Hey, lay-deee" like Jerry Lewis and walk on my ankles to my room.

"She was with me, Mrs. Green," Sophie said. "I was upset and unhappy, and Francine generously agreed to stay and comfort me." She sighed and pushed her hair back. "I have no mother, you know."

My mother patted Sophie gently on the arm. "Poor girl. Of course." She shook her head. "But next time you're upset, go to the Sisters or come to me instead of leading Francine astray. Francine has always been such a good girl, and we like her that way." My mother meant every word. She has no irony. "Now, come into the kitchen. I'm making cinnamon toast."

I couldn't believe it. I was in the clear. I smiled gratefully at Sophie as we sat down at the table. Boy, did I owe her. She winked and took a big bite of her toast, sending cinnamon and sugar spraying in all directions. "Next time we'll go see Frank Sinatra," she whispered. And I felt like I might, just might, be able to do it.

"Sister Pete," I said when I arrived at the library after school the next day, "I'm so sorry I didn't come yesterday. I got mixed up and just forgot."

I didn't mention that I hadn't been in school at all. Sister Pete is pretty modern for a nun, but not that modern.

"It's all right, Francine. We weren't busy. But . . ." She stopped and looked at me. The tight wimple pinched her cheeks together and made her face a mass of wrinkles, like a raisin or a topographical map of Bolivia. "Please don't get so distracted that you forget again. I depend on you."

"Yes, Sister, no, Sister," I said. "Shall I make it up today?" She nodded, and off I went to shelve books. I imagined Vic

Damone singing to me as I put *Saint Thomas, He Who Doubted* on the shelf after *The Little Flower: A Model for Catholic Girlhood* but before *Saint Virgil, Missionary to the Slavs.*

22

The Bum Shelter

My father goes to work, washes the car, and reads the newspaper. That's about it, except for sometimes on hot, breathless summer nights when the fan isn't enough to cool us. Then he piles us all in the Buick to go for a drive. Usually we head toward the beach, but it really doesn't matter—it's the soft summer air blowing in the windows that we want. My mother and father talk softly in the front seat, but the sound of the wind through the windows drowns out their words. In the backseat where Dolores and I sit, with Artie pressed up against one or the other of us, it's warm and heavy and quiet, like we're packed in cotton. The air blows in, my damp hair lifts off my neck, the sky darkens, and I feel like I could ride forever.

But that's only sometimes. Mostly he goes to work, washes the car, and reads the newspaper. That's why I was so surprised when he started digging around in the backyard.

"Fred, my tomatoes!" my mother said.

"Never mind tomatoes. This is more important."

"What is?"

He grinned. "It's a surprise."

In the mornings and after work, he dug and dug until there was a big hole right in our backyard. We tried guessing what it might be. A swimming pool, Dolores said. A fort, said Artie. My mother was hoping for a goldfish pond. I thought he would probably get tired of the digging and it would just stay a big hole. When we asked him about it, he repeated, "It's a surprise."

One Saturday after breakfast, he said, "Don't go yet, family. I have something to discuss with you." We all sat down again. "You know what that is in the backyard?" he asked.

"A hole," said Artie.

"Yes, a hole. And that hole may save our lives someday," he said. "Arthur, you may go and play."

"Because I knew the answer?"

"Yes, that's right."

Once Artie was gone, my father said, "The boy is too young to have to worry about the danger we're in, but I want us to be prepared. Russia has the bomb, China will be next, and we'll likely be their target. I got these from the Federal Civil Defense Administration." He held up two small mustard-yellow pamphlets: "You Can Survive the Bomb if You Know the Dangers and How to Escape Them" and "Preparing to Survive a Nuclear Attack." "President Truman says we don't know when or where the attack will come. We must be ready. I want you to read these pamphlets carefully. And this one," he said, holding up "Building the Family-Sized Atomic Safety Shelter," "will tell us how to have an A-number-one bombproof shelter in our own backyard, complete with food and water, a radio, and all necessary supplies."

A bomb shelter? Nuclear attack? A weight sat on my chest and I could hardly breathe. Mr. Bowman had said the H-bomb could mean the end of every living thing, and even if someone could survive, he wouldn't want to live in the world that was left. Was he right? Or could my father and the government really keep us safe? I didn't know.

"How much will this cost, Fred?" my mother asked.

"Doesn't matter. The protection of my family is beyond price. But we can come up with a ballpark figure." He licked the tip of his pencil and started to write on a yellow tablet. "Mattresses or sleeping bags. Bottled water. Lorraine, you make us a food list," he said, nodding to my mother. "Now, we'll need a battery-powered radio—"

"Can we have two?" Dolores asked. "What if I want to listen to something different from—"

"Dolores, the radio is for emergencies, not jitterbugging. One radio. A generator. A flashlight. First-aid kit. Air filter and exhaust pump. Geiger counter and radiation-proof suits." He licked the pencil point again. "To construct the shelter itself, we'll need cement. Steel beams. Insulation."

"Could we really live in there, Fred?" my mother asked. "What would we use for a toilet? Where would we bathe? And what would we do with garbage?"

"Will there be someplace to hang my clothes?" Dolores asked.

I jumped up. "Holy cow, Dolores. We're talking about Russia dropping a bomb on us. We're talking about living or maybe dying in a hole in the ground, and you're worried about radios and clothes! Don't be stupid."

"That's enough, Francine," my father said. "Sit down and be quiet. You too, Dolores." He licked the pencil point once more. "We'll only be in the shelter for five days. This pamphlet says radioactivity is seldom harmful, but we should wait an hour before going outside to give it a chance to die down. However, to be safe, I'm planning for us to stay in the shelter for five days."

Five days? But we'd seen in newsreels what Japan looked like after the bomb. What good would it do us to be underground for an hour or even five days? I felt sick to my stomach.

"I'll prepare a budget for building and equipping the shelter," my father said then. "Lorraine, figure out the cost of the food. You girls make a list of what you'll need—schoolbooks and essentials—I said *essentials*. I'll call another meeting when we have all the information."

"You know, Francine," Dolores said as we left the table, "I may not be a brain like you, but I'm not such an idiot that I don't worry about the bomb and stuff sometimes. I just try not to. What good does it do?"

I shrugged. "No good, I guess, but how can you stop?"

An airplane flew overhead. We both stiffened and held our breath until it passed.

Dolores and I looked at each other. We were thinking the same thing. I could see it in her eyes: *Not this time. The communists didn't blow us to bits . . . this time.*

"Come here, Frannie. Come look," Artie called from his room.

There was a Lincoln Log fortress growing on his floor. "What are you building?" I asked as I flopped down beside him.

"A place for bums to go."

"What does that mean?" I asked.

"You know, a shelter. For bums. I heard Dad talking about it. A bum shelter."

Oh, Artie! "You mean a *bomb* shelter?"

"No. Maybe. What's a bomb?"

"Well, it's like a big metal can filled with dynamite and people take it in an airplane and drop it on other people, and it blows them up."

He picked up his stuffed bear and crawled over until he was leaning against my side. "Is someone going to drop one on us? Will it be the end of the world? Will we all die? Will Chester Bear die?"

Those were good questions, and the very ones I had been thinking about ever since President Truman's speech, but I didn't tell Artie that. "No, I'm sure not. No one would do such a thing, drop bombs on other people. No, I'm sure not." I held Artie and Chester tightly.

23

April 1950

The End of the Bum Shelter

The soft summerlike air woke me up early in the morning. I stretched and reached for *Mr. Roberts*. It was taking me a very long time to read the book because I couldn't let my family see it. I was sure it wouldn't be approved at home, either.

I thought parts of the book were funny, like when one sailor got drunk and tried to bring a goat on board, but much of it was boring. The sailors stood around a lot, looking out to sea. Ensign Pulver was one of the engineering officers. He mostly stayed in his bunk reading and drinking liquor. He always said he was going to pull this trick or that trick on the captain, but he was too afraid of getting into trouble so he never did, although once by accident he made an explosion.

I felt uncomfortable. It was clear that the writer of the book and Mr. Roberts and the other sailors didn't think much of Ensign Pulver, and I was afraid I was just like him.

Where were those unplumbed depths Mr. Bowman said I had?

I put the book under my pillow, got myself a glass of orange juice, and went outside into the spring morning. There was Artie, in his cowboy pajamas, kicking dirt into the Buick-sized hole my father was digging so industriously every evening.

"Stop it, Artie! What are you doing?"

He looked up at me, his glasses all fogged up from his efforts. "Joey Manila says if you dig deep enough, you can get all the way to China. Is that true?"

"Maybe. I guess. It would have to be an awful deep hole."

"Deeper than this?" He kicked more dirt into our father's hole.

"Much deeper. Why do you want to go to China?"

"I don't. It's the commanisks. Daddy says there are commanisks in China. They could come right up this hole into our backyard and kill us." He began to kick dirt furiously into the hole again. "What's commanisks, Francine?"

I wished I could answer that for myself as well as Artie. What exactly *was* a communist? "Well, Artie," I said, "some people think communists are bad men who want to kill us. Others say they are just people who think differently from us. Or care about poor people, or like Russia or China, or refuse to say whether or not they are communists."

"Why do they want to kill us?" Artie asked. He shoved dirt into the hole with both hands. "How long will it take them to get here?"

"Oh, Artie, don't worry. Dad will never get this hole dug all the way to China." I looked at his scared little face. "Especially if we keep filling it up every morning." I joined Artie in kicking dirt into the hole. Then we sat on the edge, dangling our feet over, and ate Rice Krispies as we watched the sun rise higher in the sky.

And we did this for the next four mornings, until Artie forgot to be scared and I got tired of getting up so early.

On Saturday afternoon we met around the kitchen table again. My mother and Dolores gave my father their lists. He stretched out his hand for mine. I cleared my throat. I hadn't made a list. I doubted a bomb shelter would be of any help at all, even if we actually got around to building one, and I had decided to say so. I was going to speak up. I knew I could do it. After all, I had skipped school and spent a day of tomfoolery in Hollywood, hadn't I? I could do this.

"I don't have a list," I told him. "I think . . . maybe . . . I mean, a bomb shelter won't really do any good." His face was getting red, and my hands started to sweat. "I mean, how will five days in a hole help us if someone drops a bomb on Los Angeles?"

If this were a cartoon before the double feature, smoke would have been coming out of my father's nose. "Francine Louise Green, did you read those pamphlets I gave you on surviving the bomb?"

I nodded. The pamphlets from the government said that if a bomb fell while we were outside, we should proceed immediately to our bomb shelter. If we couldn't get there, we should hide in a building or jump into any handy ditch or gutter. In the house, we should close the windows, pull the drapes, and not use the telephone. You'd think they were being ironic—"Don't worry if an atomic bomb falls. Just jump in a ditch"—but I was pretty sure they weren't. "Yes, but—"

My father leaned toward me. "Are you telling me you know more than the government and the president?"

"No, of course not, but—"

"Are you telling me that they are wrong and *you* are right?"

I thought that actually I was, but I couldn't say so out loud. "No" was all I said.

"Then be quiet and let us get on with making plans for our safety in case the worst happens and a bomb is dropped. Is that all right with your know-it-all self?"

I nodded. Tomfoolery was one thing; arguing with my father was clearly another. Obviously I didn't have that kind of bravery.

He studied the lists he had, then wrote down columns of numbers and added them, subtracted them, turned the paper over, and started again. His face was all shiny with sweat.

Finally he said, "This may take longer to finance than I thought." He looked at Dolores and me. "Have the nuns taught you to 'duck and cover'?"

We nodded. At school we had practiced crawling under our desks and covering our heads with our hands. That way the atomic blast wouldn't harm us, the nuns said. From what I'd seen in photos and newsreels, even fifty-story buildings didn't protect people. Our little wooden desks wouldn't last a second.

"Well, that'll have to do for a while, then," my father said, wiping the sweat off his face with his handkerchief. He leaned back in his chair. "What kind of world is this, with communists threatening, spies in the government, A-bombs and H-bombs? How's a man to keep his family safe? One hour in the house with the blinds drawn. Five days in an atomic safety shelter. The government tells us that's the thing to do. But then why do they recommend radiation suits and Geiger counters? I don't know. I just don't know." His shoulders drooped, and he shook his head a few times. "How's about a martooni, Lorraine?"

I couldn't sleep that night. I kept tossing and turning, imagining President Truman and my father and even the nuns with their noses growing, like Pinocchio's. If *I* knew bombs were more dangerous than they were telling us, surely *they* knew. If they would lie about this, what else might they lie about? Maybe I was adopted. . . .

An airplane flew overhead, so close my windows rattled. My whole body tensed, waiting for the boom or bright light or blast of heat from a bomb. Was this how the people of Hiroshima felt? Or did they sleep peacefully, not knowing what was coming?

No bombs fell. I put my pillow over my head and tried to sleep.

24

An Imaginary Dinner at the Greens'

I was awakened by the sound of the bedroom door opening, little bare feet shuffling across the floor, and the *whoosh*
of a small hose being turned on.

"Mother!" I shouted. "He's doing it again!"

"What? Who?" Dolores mumbled as she turned over, but
she didn't wake up.

"Come on, Arthur," my mother whispered from the
doorway. "This is the girls' room. The bathroom is down
that way."

I jumped out of bed and turned on the light. My black
flats—$2.88 at Sears in November—sat on the floor of the
closet, wet and shiny. "Mother, look! Does he have to use my
shoes as a toilet? Can't you make him stop?"

"Don't carry on so, Francine," she said. "Wash them out
with soapy water and bleach, and dry them in the sun.
They'll be good as new in no time." She put her arm around
the still-sleeping Artie and walked him back to his room.

I took a pencil from my dresser, picked up the shoes with it, one at a time, and dropped them into the wastebasket. I would deal with them in the morning.

My mother looked in on her way back to bed. "Go back to sleep now, Francine," she said.

"Why is he peeing in our closet? It's disgusting," I said. "Having Artie for a brother is like having a life-sized Betsy Wetsy doll."

"It's not his fault. He's sleepwalking."

"Mother, if my flats are ruined and I have to get a new pair, can they be red? I'd love to have a pair of red shoes."

"Nonsense. Red shoes would be very impractical. Black you can wear with most everything. And I'm sure they'll be fine after you wash them." She stood silent a moment, then said, "I know Artie's doing this more often now, Francine. But be patient with him. I think something's bothering him."

Of course something was bothering him. Bombs and communists and creepy Joey Manila. He wasn't even six yet. He shouldn't have to be worried about such things.

After all that, I naturally couldn't go back to sleep. What a family. What did I ever do wrong to deserve such a family? If I had my way, I thought, the Dinner at the Greens' movie would have a scene like this:

MOTHER *(coming in from the kitchen with a big platter)*: Here we are, family: T-bone steaks, corn on the cob, raisin bread, and chocolate cream pie.

Be sure to take seconds. There is plenty.

FRANCINE: Thank you, Mother. But tell me, where is Dolores? I do not see her here at the table.

FATHER: We have decided to send Dolores to boarding school at the North Pole. After she graduates, she will go straight to her job on a llama farm in Bolivia. The bedroom is all yours now.

MOTHER: Yes, we thought we'd remodel it any way you like, dear. Just tell us.

FATHER: And we are hiring a nanny for Arthur so you don't have to watch him all the time. We know you have more important things to do.

MOTHER: We're getting him a bedpan and a lock for his door. You will have no more visits in the night.

FATHER: Now we'd like to know more about you. Tell us, Francine, who is your favorite singer?

MOTHER: What will fashions be like next year? We value your opinion.

FATHER: And what do you think of the world situation now that Joseph Stalin has decided Russia will not make a bomb and has called all communists home?

MOTHER: Yes, tell us.

FATHER: Speak up, Francine.

MOTHER: By the way, Montgomery Clift just moved in next door.

FATHER: And your hair looks lovely.

MOTHER: More pie, Francine?

Fade Out

I fell asleep smiling.

25

Class-Visit Day at the Sinless Academy for the Maidenly

"You gotta hear this," boomed Jacob Mandelbaum, pounding into the Bowmans' living room, where Sophie and I were playing checkers. "Harry, come. You just gotta hear this." He sat down on one end of the sofa and stuck a big black cigar into his mouth.

Mr. Bowman came in with cups of coffee for himself and Mr. Mandelbaum and Cokes for us. Mr. Mandelbaum took a big sip, lit his cigar, and said, "I went to the baseball game yesterday—the home opener, Stars versus the Portland Beavers. Got my beer and my foot-long and started looking around to see who's in the stands. I see George Burns and Gracie Allen, Clark Gable, Gary Cooper, Elizabeth Taylor, even. Lots of Hollywood big shots.

"Suddenly a cheer goes up. They're comin' out, Kelleher, Stevens, Woods, Sauer, all the guys. Our Hollywood Stars, winners of the Pacific Coast League pennant in 1949, rah-rah and ready to go, and—ya gotta listen to this. . . ." He puffed furiously on his cigar, and smoke wreathed his head. "They're in *shorts,* like Cub Scouts or chorus girls. Short pants and knee socks. Ya shoulda seen it, Harry.

"Everybody was yelling 'Nice legs ya got, Frankie,' and 'Ain't ya cold, sweetheart?' One guy stood on his seat and hollered, 'What's next? Shavin' your legs?'" Mr. Mandelbaum laughed for a minute and then slapped the side of his head. "First cheerleaders, now short pants. What Joe Knucklehead in the Stars organization makes these decisions?"

Shorts made me think of bathing suits and bathing beauties, so I blurted out, "Miss America."

They all looked at me in silent surprise and then burst into laughter. "Miss America!" Mr. Mandelbaum shouted. "The girl's a comedian, a regular Jack Benny."

My face grew hot at all the attention, but I have to admit I kind of liked it. After all, I would have to get used to such things if I was going to be a movie star.

The next day was class-visit day at All Saints School for Girls, when students spent time in the classrooms they'd be in next year. Except for us eighth graders, who would be freshmen in high school and have a different nun and a different room for each subject. I'd still be going to All Saints, but the high school was in the new building, connected to the old one by a corridor with locked doors on both sides. Like the Iron Curtain that divided Eastern Europe from the West, that corridor kept us strictly separate. I don't know if that was to protect the younger students from the high school girls or vice versa.

It was a little scary to think about next year—not just

having a new building and new teachers, but being so old. Being a little girl was much easier. I never had to worry about things like bombs and communists, like my expanding chest, like boys. I'd been scared, sure, by fireworks and loud music and clowns. Especially clowns. Clowns have weird painted faces and are noisy and like people looking at them. There must be something very wrong with clowns. But I never had to worry about being blown up by someone with a bomb who hates America.

"Welcome, seventh graders," Sister Basil said as we eighth graders scootched over to make room for the visitors. She began to pair us up. "No," she said to a redheaded girl who was about to sit with Sophie, "not there. We don't want you to pick up bad habits."

So some of the seventh graders stood at the back of the classroom because there were no more desks to share, and Sophie, alone of all the eighth graders, sat by herself. She pushed her hair back behind her ears and sat up straight and tall.

The girl who shared my desk smelled like moth balls and the onion sandwiches she ate for lunch. Her hair was tightly braided and, even on this warm spring day, her sweater tightly buttoned. I'd seen her around the playground, sitting by herself, kicking in the dirt. Nobody liked her. Still, I thought I would be friendly and tell her things and help her adjust to eighth grade and Sister Basil, but she looked down at her desk and not at me even once.

"Let's see how well you new girls know your catechism,"

Sister said. "You," she said, pointing to a girl behind me. "What do we mean when we say God is eternal?"

The girl stood. "When we say God is eternal," she said, "we mean that He always was and always will be and always remains the same."

Sister Basil nodded. "What do we mean by the Blessed Trinity?" she asked a girl standing in the back.

"When we say the Blessed Trinity, we mean one and the same God in three divine persons."

Sister looked slowly around the room. "You," she said to my desk mate. "What is your name?"

"Mumble, mumble," said the girl, looking down at the desk.

"Stand up," I whispered to her. She shuffled to her feet and rubbed her runny nose but still did not look up.

"What is your name?" repeated Sister Basil.

"Mumble mumble Patsy mumble," the girl said.

"Well, Patsy, tell us what holy chrism is."

Patsy said nothing.

We'd been asked these same questions for eight years now. I knew all the correct responses. I wrote the answer on a piece of paper and shoved it toward her. "Psst, Patsy," I whispered, "look." But she just stared down at her feet.

Sister continued. "What do we mean by the Passion of Our Lord Jesus Christ? How does the Church remit the temporal punishment due to sins?" Her voice got louder. "What is the superabundant satisfaction of the Blessed Virgin Mary and the saints?"

I was afraid to "Psst" any louder, because it might attract

Sister's attention, so I just sat there. Patsy didn't move a muscle. I could see tears hit the floor at her feet. "I dunno," she said.

Sister Basil's face shone red with irritation, and then she smiled. It appeared she and her trash can had already found next year's victim. She didn't even have to wait until September. Lucky Sister Basil. Poor Patsy.

"What *do* we mean by the Passion of Our Lord Jesus Christ?" Sophie asked on the way home. "What kind of passion?"

It hadn't occurred to me that someone might not know. "Passion as in suffering and dying," I said. "Like Jesus did. Or martyrs. Or really strong religious feelings like saints have."

"I always thought saints were meek, obedient, and quiet, above it all. The opposite of passionate."

"Are you kidding? Think about martyrs who got burned at the stake because they loved God so much. Or worried about Jesus until they bled or fainted or foamed at the mouth." I got up to pull the cord for our stop.

"Yuck," Sophie said. "Would you ever do that?"

"I'm not a saint."

"But can you imagine feeling something so deeply that you'd do something that strange?"

"Not me. I might get into trouble." I couldn't imagine caring about anything so much that I wouldn't worry about trouble. Not me. Joan of Arc, maybe—so passionate and brave and un-Francine-like. But not me.

I was invited for Chinese takeout at the Bowmans' on

Sunday. My mother says it's a waste of money to pay a restaurant for food when she can cook perfectly well, and my father won't have anything Chinese in the house because of communism, so I'd never eaten Chinese food before. This was quite an occasion for me.

"Chop suey, Francine?" said Sophie as she passed me something in brown gravy. "Egg foo yung?" Something else in brown gravy.

Actually, both dishes tasted a lot like something my mother would cook. I didn't say that to Sophie. She would know it wasn't a compliment.

After a few mouthfuls of brown gravy, I went into the kitchen for a glass of water. I hoped the Chinese had other things to eat besides this or they'd be invading America for the food.

When I returned to the table, Sophie was holding a spoonful of strawberry Jell-O and saying, "So I asked her, 'Where in the Bible is there a rule about wearing a hat to church?' and she said, 'You think you're so superior and smart, but you're not. You're going to Hell, and how smart is that?' I tell you, those girls have no brains. I mean, do they think God really cares who wears a hat? Don't these questions occur to anyone else?"

"Harry? Sophie? Hello?" someone called from the door.

"Come in, Jacob," Mr. Bowman said. "Grab a plate and join the feast."

Mr. Mandelbaum came in through the open door and sat down. Ignoring the food, he ran his hands through his hair, leaving it sticking straight up. "The FBI had me in for questioning again, Harry," he said. "Why are they hounding me? I voted for Harry Truman, and I think Stalin is a stinker. I'm a good citizen. Why can they do this? Shouldn't I be protected from—"

"What do you mean, protected?" Mr. Bowman asked. He shook his head slowly. "Remember, this is the country that imprisoned a hundred thousand of its citizens because they were Japanese, that makes its Negro citizens in the South use separate rest rooms, restaurants, and schools. There is little protection here for those who are different, especially now when everyone is so afraid." He reached over and touched Mr. Mandelbaum's arm. "I'm worried about you, Jacob."

"The worst of it is, I can't work," Mr. Mandelbaum said. "First time since I was fourteen. Stage, screen, radio, I've done it all. And now no one will touch Jacob Mandelbaum. Or even Jack Mann." He smiled sadly and patted his stomach. "I might get a little hungry from not eating, but I could stand to lose a few pounds. It's my work and my friends I couldn't stand to lose. What else do I have?"

"Baseball," I whispered. I was scared to death by all this talk, but I wanted to give poor Mr. Mandelbaum some comfort.

"Ah, Francine, my darling, baseball, yes. Even the FBI can't take that away." He was silent for a moment. I could see his hands trembling. "So tell me, Harry," he asked in a small voice so unlike his regular bellow, "I'm really in danger? They can do this, ask me about my politics? Question my friends? Keep me from working? I broke no law."

Mr. Bowman got up and closed the front door. "It's happening all over. We're supposed to have rights—the right to work, to teach, to circulate ideas without interference, to protest over bad laws—but it doesn't seem to matter. Be careful, Jacob. Be very careful."

Fear had come into the Bowmans' house like fog, silent and clammy, making me shiver. None of us wanted strawberry Jell-O after that.

26

May 1950

May Day

We were standing in the hallway, preparing for the May procession in honor of Mary, the Blessed Virgin. The large statue in the vestibule had been scrubbed and polished until it shone. The nuns walked among us, distributing flowers to each girl, to be laid at the feet of the Mother of God, whose month this was.

Susan Murphy had been elected May Queen, but when she climbed up on the ladder in rehearsal to crown the statue, Sister Basil finally got a good look at the riot of flowers on her uniform skirt and unelected her. In her place Sister appointed—no, not Mary Agnes, thank you—Florence Bush. Her pale face shone as she took her place at the end of the procession.

The rest of us lined up by height. Sophie stood a few girls ahead of me. I was shocked. I had always thought she was much taller. Had I grown a lot this year, or had Sophie always been shorter than I and I never noticed because she seemed so strong and invincible? I heard her call to Sister Basil, "Sister Rott . . . uh . . . Basil, may I ask you something?"

"Not now, Miss Bowman," Sister said.

"Not ever, Miss Bowman," I thought.

But Sophie persisted. "It's important and has been weighing on my mind."

Sister gave her a reluctant wave of permission.

"Sister, is it wrong of me to participate in this event if I'm not sure I believe in God? Is it a sin or a sacrilege or something?"

We all stood as still as the Virgin's statue. Not believe in God? Catholic girls aren't allowed not to believe in God. It had never occurred to me to question His existence.

Sister did not say a word, so Sophie continued. "If I don't believe in God, and I'm not sure whether or not I do, then I couldn't believe in His Holy Mother, and I wouldn't want to offend or insult people who do believe by acting as if—"

"Miss Bowman," Sister said, hissing the s through her teeth, "that is enough. Go back to the classroom."

Sophie went, muttering "Sorry" to me as she passed.

Not believe in God? I didn't know exactly what I thought about God myself. I mean, He wasn't doing such a good job of running the world, letting people invent the bomb and be cruel to one another and kill one another, but I liked thinking *someone* was in charge.

When I was little, I thought that God was like Santa Claus, all white and rosy, taking care of us and giving us whatever we needed. Now sometimes He seemed to me like

Sister Basil in a beard, punishing people and damning them to Hell. Other times, when the world didn't seem so bad, I pictured God as Mr. Bowman, the way he looked on Saturdays in his baggy corduroy pants, pruning his roses and humming his happy song. That was the God I loved, the one who tended His people like Mr. Bowman tended his roses.

But whatever God I pictured, I always believed He was there. I couldn't imagine not believing at all.

Sister Basil clapped her hands, and we girls began to sing "On This Day, O Beautiful Mother" as we shuffled forward to lay our flowers at the feet of the Mother of the God who might or might not exist.

When we returned to the classroom, Sophie was sitting quietly at her desk, staring straight ahead. Sister Basil did not acknowledge her but walked to the front of the room while we all took our seats. She stood looking at us for a moment, and then she spoke. "They are punished in Hell," she said, "who die in mortal sin. I want you to imagine the worst pain you ever felt. Now multiply it by a thousand, a million, a million million. That is the pain of Hell." She paused a minute to let that sink in. "And even worse than the pain is the knowledge that it will never ever end."

She paced up and down, swinging her rosary. "Girls, such are the wages of sin. Do not think, 'I will confess and repent before I die and thus be saved from Hell.' It may not happen. No one knows the manner or the hour of his death. You say, 'Oh, what does it matter if I miss Mass just this one time?' or 'This meat looks too delicious to pass up even if it is Friday,' or 'I will let him kiss me even though it is wrong for it will make him like me,' and the next day you are hit by a bus and spend the rest of eternity in Hell."

No one said a word. The only one likely to interrupt at this point was Sophie, and she was sitting straight and silent.

"The consequences of sin are the pains of Hell," Sister continued. "And the worst sins, the unpardonable sins, are doubt, denial, despair—denying not only the goodness of God but His very existence. There is no forgiveness for that.

"Today one of you started on the road to Hell. Saving your souls is the most important job I have, and in her case, it appears, I am failing."

She stopped and looked around. We made not a sound. A dark shadow had settled over the classroom, and I could almost smell sulfur and ashes and the singed hair of the damned. "Class dismissed," Sister said.

Sophie and I grabbed seats in the bus. "Do you believe all those things Sister said about Hell?" she asked me.

"I guess so," I told her. "All priests and nuns talk about Hell, although only Sister Basil is so, well, descriptive. Nobody who died has come back to tell us for sure."

I used to think the best thing to do would be to go to confession and then walk out of the church right in front of a bus in order to be sure to die without sin and avoid the torments of Hell. But if you did it deliberately, it would be suicide, a mortal sin, a fast ticket to damnation. One would have to innocently wander in front of the bus, truly expecting not to be hit and killed, and then just be lucky.

"What about God?" Sophie asked me. "Do you believe in God?"

"Well, sure, I believe in God. I know there's no proof, but still I believe. Otherwise it all seems so confused and chaotic. I guess that's what they mean by faith." Sophie started to say something, but I went on. "Sophie, I *want* there to be a God, so don't argue with me."

"If there is no God," Sophie said, "there is no Hell, so I'm going to pray there is no God."

"Who will you pray to?"

She shook her head. "I don't know. It's very puzzling."

27

Mother's Day at Forest Lawn

Artie grabbed me as soon as Sophie and I walked into the kitchen. "Francine, a clown tried to eat me!"

Even feeling as I did about clowns, I wasn't sure I believed him. "How? Where?"

"Daddy took me miniature golfing and I hit my ball and it was supposed to go in the clown's mouth, but it went far away somewhere instead and I couldn't find it and when I looked by the clown I tripped and my foot went in his mouth and he wouldn't let go." Artie jumped up and down with excitement. "Firemen came and killed the clown with hammers and axes and finally he let me go and he died."

"Are you okay, Artie? Are you hurt?"

"No, but we can't play miniature golf there anymore. The man said."

Ever since Artie's sleepwalking episodes had become more frequent, my father worried that Artie was becoming a sissy. "Too many females in this boy's life," he said. "Time to make a man out of him." And he began a campaign.

The week before, they had gone fishing at the pond in Griffith Park. Artie didn't catch any fish, but he caught a dog. His hook got caught in the curly hair of a tiny poodle and they couldn't get it out. When my father took his pocket-knife and cut the dog's hair to free it, her owner cried. Then Artie cried and they came home. It seemed to me that Artie's road to manhood would not be easy.

"What are you doing now?" I asked him, examining the mess at the kitchen table.

He climbed up onto a chair. "I'm making a card. For Mommy. For Mother's Day. See?" He showed it to me and then stuck it under Sophie's nose.

"Take a hike, squirt," she said, brushing glitter off her face.

"It's very pretty, Artie," I said. "Go and hide it so Mother doesn't see it until Sunday.

"Sophie," I said to her after Artie left, "you could be nicer to him. He's just a little kid."

"You know I don't like little kids."

It was more than that, I suddenly realized. "You don't much like anybody except in big groups, like 'the poor' or 'the persecuted' or 'those who fight fascism.' People separately you don't like. Come on, admit it."

"That's ridiculous. I like Jacob Mandelbaum. And Harry." I raised one eyebrow at her as she stopped to think of some-body else. "And I used to like you," she said.

"And I like you," I said, "anyway." I brushed glitter off

my uniform skirt. "Wasn't Artie's card cute, with that crooked heart and the glue all smeared around? Do you remember the cards you made in school? Glitter angels on the Christmas cards. Drawing around your hand to make turkeys for Thanksgiving. Mother's Day cards made out of doilies and paper flowers. Remember?"

"What I remember is the vacant lot near school where I threw the Mother's Day cards every year because I didn't have a mother to give them to."

"Sorry, Soph. I forgot."

She waved my apology away. "I got used to it. I thought once about giving the cards to Harry, since he's the closest thing to a mother I've ever had. But he's not very good at mother things, like cooking or having birthday parties or saying 'You're not going anywhere until you polish your shoes, young lady.' So I just threw them away."

"Is it kind of lonesome, not celebrating Mother's Day when the rest of the world does?"

"Jeeps, Francine, of course we celebrate. It's Mother's Day." She tucked her hair behind her ears in that way of hers. "Each year we plant another rosebush in the yard. Harry says my mother loved roses almost as much as she loved him. This year after pancakes at the Pig and Whistle, we're going to hear Beethoven's Fifth Symphony at the Hollywood Bowl. What are you doing for your mother?"

"Who knows?" I said. Actually, I did know, but I was embarrassed to tell Sophie, who was going to the Hollywood Bowl.

"Can I stay for dinner tonight?" Sophie asked.

"Dinner at the Greens'? Why would you want to do that?"

"I like it here."

"You won't when you hear what we're having for dinner. Liver."

"I like liver," said Sophie.

"Oh nausea." I poked her in the ribs. "Come on, we'll ask my mother. I'm sure she'll say yes, but then you'll have to eat her terrible food."

"You know, Francine, you're pretty unfair to your mother."

"Ye gods, Sophie, what do you mean?"

"I mean she's your mother and she takes care of you and wipes your face with a cool cloth when you're sick and tries to cook things you would like. She's sweet and nice, and all you do is complain about her."

"She's sweet and nice to *you,* but if she were *your* mother, you'd know what I mean."

Sophie was quiet for a minute and then said, "Maybe."

Sunday was Mother's Day. My mother wore a new hat to church. Navy with a veil and white paper flowers. She made my father go to Mass with us. Usually he spends Sunday mornings asleep in the lawn chair. He says that God is just as likely to be in our backyard as in a building in West Los Angeles.

I myself like going to Mass. It's kind of like a movie or a play starring Jesus and Mary and the saints, with costumes and music. My favorite part is the ringing of the church bells. Sometimes on clear, still mornings, I can hear them from my bed. The bells are the best thing about Sunday morning, besides Mass, no school, and pancakes with blueberry syrup from Knott's Berry Farm.

After Mass we ate cheese and crackers and carrot sticks because we had fasted for Holy Communion. We ate them in the car on the way to Forest Lawn. Yes, Forest Lawn. The cemetery. That's where my mother likes to go for special occasions, the cemetery. She enjoys seeing where the movie stars are buried. I may be crazy about movie stars, but I draw the line at dead ones.

To be honest, Forest Lawn is a lot more than a cemetery. It's like a very clean, quiet city, with churches and museums, trees and statues and ponds. Only the people are all dead.

We parked the car and got out—all except Dolores, who stayed behind to sulk because she hadn't been allowed to go to the Brown Derby Restaurant with Wally and his mother.

There were plenty of living people in Forest Lawn that day, putting flowers on their mothers' graves. They walked slowly between the stones, talking quietly to each other. But my mother ran and shouted. "Here," she called as we got to the crest of a hill, "here's Tom Mix. And there, Jean Harlow. And look, Carole Lombard!" She cried a little then because of the tragic way Carole Lombard died, in an airplane crash when she was traveling the country to sell war bonds. My mother sold bonds during the war too. She still wears a baggy gray suit she made out of an old suit of my father's and used the money she saved to buy war bonds. She calls it "the suit that helped win the war."

"Fred," my mother called, "here's Humphrey Bogart's mother!"

Holy cow. I sat down under a tree and just waited for my mother to stop embarrassing me. I watched her running from grave to grave, her hair springing loose from her bun and curling around her face. Her face was rosy with joy and the sun. Suddenly I was feeling about her the way you are supposed to feel about your mother on Mother's Day. I smiled at that and lay down in the coolness of the grass.

When we were all in the car again, she said, "Now, Fred, I would like to go out to a restaurant for lunch." My mother said that. My penny-pinching mother who clipped coupons from the magazines at the dentist's office, reused waxed paper, and canned her own tomatoes. A new hat *and* out to eat. What was getting into her? If I didn't know her so well, I'd think she had a boyfriend or something.

"Blue blazes, Lorraine," my father said. "I'm not made of money."

"And not the Tail of the Pup, either. Someplace where we can sit down." She smiled. "And I might even have a cocktail."

"Blue blazes," my father said again.

28

Father Chuckie and Sister Pete

Susan was back in school after her forced vacation for drawing flowers on her uniform skirt. Sister nodded as Susan, in a fresh, clean, undecorated skirt, took her seat.

"Holy cow, Susan," I said, "did you have to get a new skirt? Did your father blow his top?"

Susan smiled and pointed to the weasely Weslia Babchuk, whose skirt was a familiar riot of flowers. "Sister will never think to check what Weslia is wearing, and then when she forgets all about my skirt, I'll take it back again."

"But how did you get the weasely Weslia to agree?"

"It's amazing how valuable a cute brother can be," Susan said.

"Scooter the drip? And weasely Weslia? I'm shocked."

"People change," Susan said, waving to Weslia, who winked at her. I saw Susan fingering the fabric of Weslia's skirt, clearly imagining how much better it would look with a few roses and daisies drawn on it.

After recess the new assistant pastor at Saint Mel's came to school to introduce himself. His name is Father Charles, but it was Chuckie when he was a teenager and visited his grandparents next door to us. Chuckie was there every weekend, working on his car, singing dirty lyrics to holy hymns, and saying "hubba hubba" whenever a female walked by.

Father Chuckie is young and very handsome, so the girls in my class think he's drooly. That's because he never held *them* upside down over the storm drain. He told us he was there for all of us young people, and if we ever had any questions or problems, we could come to him.

"Could we talk to you about sins of the flesh?" Susan asked.

Father Chuckie blushed but said, "Yes, when you're old enough."

"We're old enough now," Susan went on. "Why, I—"

"That will do, Susan," Sister said.

Sophie raised her hand and Father Chuckie nodded to her. "Well, Father," she said, "I would like to know if priests are allowed—"

"Thank you, Sophie. That's enough," said Sister. "Mary Agnes, perhaps *you* have a question for Father."

The Perfect and Admirable Mary Agnes Malone stood up slowly and smoothed down her skirt. "Father, could you recommend suitable readings for a girl who aspires to enter the Holy Sisterhood?"

Father Chuckie beamed. "Yes, yes, come see me. I'll be happy to instruct you. And any other of you girls who are considering a life of service to God." Mary Agnes sat down again.

I took a deep breath. "Father," I said, rising slowly to my feet, "could I maybe come talk to you about communists and the government and the FBI? It's all so confusing and—"

"Thank you, Francine," Sister Basil said, "but Father meant he will talk to you about matters of religion and morals. I'll tell you what you need to know about the evils of communism."

"But Sister—"

"Sit down, Francine," Sister said.

I sat.

Every day now I heard Walter Winchell on the radio talk about secret communists in this country. Hedda Hopper's newspaper column warned us daily that some writer or actor or newspaperman was "pink." Every day I saw newspapers and magazines telling us that the communists wanted our country and its children. They told us to be vigilant, to watch and listen for subversive talk, to turn in our neighbors or even our families if they seemed suspicious. And the result was what was happening to Jacob Mandelbaum.

And Sophie. The other girls all called her "comrade" and marched like soldiers behind her. *I* knew she wasn't a communist, but she wouldn't try to convince them otherwise. "And if I were, what would it matter?" Sophie asked me when I brought it up at lunch. "Not all communists are evil or planning to overthrow the government." She took a bite of her bologna sandwich. "Besides, every freedom fighter has suffered the abuse of those who do not understand."

"But you're not fighting for freedom," I said to her. "You fight for the right to play the radio, to ask questions about God and nuns in underwear, and to say what you really think in school essays."

"Same thing," said Sophie. She wadded up her lunch bag and threw it across three tables into the trash can.

I felt a little dizzy, as if the earth had tilted a bit on its axis. Talking to Sophie often made me feel like that.

"I can't just be quiet and let wrong things happen," she continued. "Even little wrong things. I want to make a difference in this world. Don't you?"

"I don't know, Soph. Sometimes I just want to get out alive." We laughed. "You know what I mean. I just want to live my life without any problems, without getting into any trouble."

"I don't think that's possible," she said.

"Well, at least I can try."

After school I thought about Sophie while I worked in the library. I needed to talk to someone about her, and Sister Pete was right here. She was kind and a good listener. I would take the chance. I put *Stories of the Popes for the Primary Grades* in its place on the shelf and walked over to Sister Pete. I cleared my throat about seventeen times but said nothing.

"You will injure your vocal cords doing that, Francine," Sister Pete said. "What is it?"

"I just wondered whether . . . I mean . . . is it—"

"Francine!"

"Sister, is it right, you know, about Sophie? How she's treated?"

Sister Pete studied me for a moment. "And how is she treated?"

"The other girls tease her. And no one will be friends with her."

"Indeed, that is not how All Saints girls should behave, but perhaps Sophie brings some of it on herself. I don't see her making an effort to be friends with the other girls."

I had thought about that. "I think Sophie likes being an outsider. She thinks it makes her . . . noble. But still it must hurt when the other girls make fun of her and call her names, even though she says it doesn't." I hesitated before going on but then plunged ahead. This could mean real trouble. "And Sister Basil doesn't help. She doesn't encourage the other girls to be nice to Sophie. In fact, Sister herself kind of . . . you know . . . sort of picks on Sophie and punishes her whenever Sophie opens her mouth."

"Francine, you and I both know Sophie deliberately provokes Sister."

I felt deflated. I'd hoped Sister Pete would take Sophie's side or at least try to understand her. "She's just speaking her mind."

"There is a time and place for everything, and Sister Basil's classroom is neither the time nor the place for speaking one's mind." Sister Pete patted the chair next to her and I sat down. "I know Sister Basil seems harsh and unfair sometimes. But each nun is different, just as each person is

different. Sister Basil expects more quiet obedience and less
. . . well, liveliness from her girls. She is our principal, and
we must honor and obey her."

"Maybe you could talk to Sister Bas—"

Sister Pete put up her hand. "I don't have the right to do
that." She smiled. "Nor the courage." She was silent for a
moment. "Sister Basil will not change, but Sophie can. Much
of what Sophie suffers is the result of her own behavior. She
can change that, and indeed, it is her responsibility to do
so."

Sister leaned back and put her clasped hands behind the
white bib of her habit. "Until then, perhaps her sufferings
can bring her closer to Jesus if she bears the taunts and pun-
ishments gladly, as He bore the cross. Talk to her about it,
Francine."

"Yes, Sister," I said.

Should I talk to Sophie? I wondered as I bounced home
on the bus. I knew I myself had told her to be quiet and
accept things, but now that advice just didn't seem right.
Sophie needed someone to defend her and not just tell her
to change or accept things gladly.

I thought Sister Basil was mean and unfair and Sister
Pete was wrong. I couldn't help it. I did. I just hoped thinking that was not too bad a sin.

29

In Sister's Office

Some days later, Mr. Bowman and Jacob Mandelbaum were sitting on the Bowmans' front porch when we got there after school. They were so quiet, I could hear the ice cubes tinkle in their glasses.

"Hi, Mr. Mandelbaum," Sophie said.

"How's my girl? No more trouble at school, I hope," he said.

"Everything's fine," she said, giving him a quick hug.

We sat down on the steps. "What's going on?" Sophie asked.

"The FBI again," Mr. Bowman said. "That's them, parked in front of the Martins'." He pointed to a dark-green Ford with two men in the front seat. "They followed Jacob here."

My heart thumped. The FBI was right across the street. I was pretty sure this was "getting involved."

"They broke into my house while I was gone, searched for what-I-don't-know, threw my clothes on the floor. And my books," Mr. Mandelbaum said in a small voice so very different from his usual boom. "Now they're here."

"Are you sure it was the FBI," I asked in a whisper, "and not burglars?"

He nodded. "Sure I'm sure. They're after me. Me! I'm for beer and baseball and enough to eat for everybody; I'm against Brussels sprouts, phonies, stuffed shirts, and government goons. For that I'm called a criminal, and they take away my work. And now . . ."

"The FBI wants to make a deal with Jacob," Mr. Bowman told us. "If he will confess that the communists used him and give the names of others who might be or have been or have known communists, he'll be excused."

"Name names, they said," said Mr. Mandelbaum, "and they'll get off my back. Squeal—that's what they want me to do. Squeal. I would never. What should I do? What should I do?"

His eyes filled with tears. My heart thumped again. Adults were supposed to be sure and strong. I didn't want to see them cry.

I stood up. "I have to go home."

"Oh, Francine, please, stay," Mr. Bowman said. "We shouldn't be frightening you like this. I forget, all girls aren't battle veterans like my Sophie. Sit. We'll talk about something else."

"It's all right, Mr. Bowman. I do have to go home."

My father was reading the newspaper when I got there. "Dad?" I asked.

He looked up. "What's wrong, Frannie?"

How could he tell? Did I sound as scared as I felt? "Mr. Bowman's friend, Jacob Mandelbaum, said the FBI—"

He interrupted me. "I told you, I don't want you to get involved in all that political talk. You're much too young to be worried about it."

"But the FBI is investigating him," I said. "Did you know that they do that to ordinary people?"

He folded his newspaper and put it on his lap. "The FBI must know something. Where there's smoke, there's fire."

"Dad, do you know that some people call labor unions communist?"

He shook his head. "That's ridiculous. Union men are good Americans, fighting for the rights of the working man, for fair pay and decent working conditions. How much more American can you be?"

I pushed on, hoping to get more answers before he became impatient and grouchy. "Isn't that what communists do—fight for the rights of the working man? And if people are wrong about unions, could they be wrong about communists?"

"I don't have all the answers, Francine," he said, running his hands through his hair. Holy cow, I thought, he doesn't have all the answers and he's admitting it and he's *still* not grouchy! I was astonished. "It's complicated," he continued. "First Russia was on our side against the Nazis. Now we hear that the same country, same people, are evil and out to destroy freedom in our country like they did in theirs. I just don't know. But I do know I want real Americans in charge of America, not some stooges sent by Russia. That's what I know." He picked up the newspaper and opened it. "The world is all so different now. How can anyone keep up?" He shook his head again. "It's a different world, Francine. A different world."

I went into my room and lay on the bed. Holy cow. My father just talked to me like I was a real person. And I liked it.

From outside came the sounds of Artie and his friends playing hide-and-seek. Their shouts and their laughter rang in the spring evening. I envied them. They sounded so innocent and out of place in this world where we were all trying to destroy one another.

"Francine, come to my office after school," Sister Basil said before church history the next day. "I would like to talk with you."

My heart fell into my saddle shoes. In all my eight years at No Sinners, I had never been called to the principal's office. What could I have done? I was sure she hadn't seen me stick my tongue out at Mary Agnes during catechism.

Oh no. Could Sister Pete have squealed on me? If so, I was dead.

All afternoon my thoughts were jumbled. I couldn't concentrate on anything. What was going to happen to me?

After school I stood outside her office door and tried to slow my breathing down, preparing to enter the lair of the evil Sister Basil the Rotten. I knocked finally, very softly, hoping she wouldn't hear me and I could go safely home.

"Come in," she called.

I went in. On this rainy May day the office was filled

with a cool, green light. Sister Basil motioned me to a chair facing her desk. A large cross with a bronze dying Jesus hung over her head where every visitor would have to stare straight at it.

Sister's desk was large and wooden, its top bare—not one scrap of paper, not a pen or paper clip. No books, no picture, no vase of flowers. Just the bare, polished surface that reflected Sister Basil's scowling face.

"Don't slouch, Francine," she said.

I stood up straighter.

"Sit down, Francine," she said.

I sat.

In movies people's knees knock with fear, and I expected that mine would. They didn't, but my mouth was awfully dry. I held my breath as long as I could and watched her carefully, hoping she wouldn't smile.

Sister said nothing. We just sat there in silence until I thought I would have to scream.

"Francine," Sister said finally, folding her hands carefully in the very center of her desk, "I am concerned about you. You are aware of the dangers of occasions of sin—people and circumstances that can tempt you into sinning . . ."

My breath whooshed out. Sister Pete had not betrayed me. But what was Sister Basil talking about? The *True Confessions* magazine Gert had let me read at recess yesterday?

Sister cleared her throat. "When you are young," she said, "every day, every minute, every action and emotion, is critical. You are making choices, going in one direction or another. It is my duty to watch over you girls, to attend to your spiritual and your temporal welfare, and keep you from making dangerous decisions."

She unfolded her hands and leaned back in her chair. "I care about you," she went on, "and when I see you in danger of making unsuitable choices, it is my duty to instruct you—to make sure that your activities are worthwhile, your entertainments are wholesome, and your friends are the right sort, that they are positive influences on you and help you choose the right direction."

Cared about me? She did? Was she being ironic? And did she mean I should be friends with the Perfect and Admirable Mary Agnes Malone? That would never work, no matter what Sister thought. Why, I'd rather drop out of school, jump into a pool full of sharks, let red ants crawl over my naked body . . .

Sister was still talking when I tuned her back in. ". . . unruly and disruptive, and her father is politically suspicious. This is why it would be better if you ended your friendship right now, before—"

"Sister, do you mean *Sophie?*" I asked out loud in a voice more squeak than not.

"Of course, Francine. Whom else have we been talking about?"

Sophie? Why, she wasn't unruly or disruptive. Well, I guess she was. But she was my friend. She was smart and interesting. She needed me, and I learned so much from her. Sister didn't see that side of her.

"It's for the best, Francine," Sister said. She nodded

toward the door. "You may go." I got to my feet. "You will think about what I said, won't you?"

"Yes, Sister," I whispered as I opened the door. I knew what she meant: "You will do what I say, won't you?" And I knew that it wasn't really a question.

30

Serious Trouble for Mr. Roberts,
Mr. Mandelbaum, and Sophie

Mr. Roberts is dead. I absolutely loathe Mr. Thomas Heggen, who wrote the book, and made me love Mr. Roberts and be happy for him when he was finally transferred to a ship in the middle of the war, and then, with just a few pages left, killed him off.

I put the book back under my pillow. I'd finish it later when I wasn't so sad.

The day started out bad and got worse. Sophie wasn't at school, the Perfect and Admirable Mary Agnes Malone got 100 percent on her religion quiz, and I fell and skinned my knee at recess. After my shift at the library, I missed the five-thirty bus and had to wait ages for another.

Sophie was waiting for me when I got off the bus. "Sophie!" I said, grabbing her arm. "How long have you been waiting here? Why weren't you in school today? I hate it when—"

"Francine, listen," she said in a funny, tight voice. She

wiped her red nose with the back of her hand. "Jacob Mandelbaum is dead." Dead? That kind, funny man with the smelly cigars? "It's so awful. He shot himself. In his car. At the beach in Santa Monica."

My eyes prickled. "*Shot* himself? But why?"

"Why do you think? They were hounding him, the FBI and who knows who else. He couldn't do what they wanted him to, and he couldn't see a way out, so he killed himself." She snuffled. I dug my handkerchief out of my pocket and gave it to her. She blew her nose loudly.

We were silent as we walked. Mr. Mandelbaum had shot himself. Suicide. Straight to Hell. That's what the church taught, anyway. Maybe it was different for Jews. I hoped so. This was one of the times I preferred to think God was more like Mr. Bowman than like Sister Basil. God and Mr. Mandelbaum could sit on a cloud together and talk about baseball.

I took a deep breath. "When is his funeral?" I asked Sophie. "Are you going?"

"Mr. M always said he wouldn't want a funeral. He wanted his friends to go watch the Hollywood Stars and have a beer and a cigar. So that's what they're going to do." She snuffled again. "Not me, though. I don't want to laugh and be happy. I'm going to stay home and make up plots against the FBI."

"Come on in," I said when we reached my house.

"Can't. Got to go." She gave me a quick hug and ran off.

"Francine," my mother called from the kitchen as I entered. "You're late. Dinner is ready." I dumped my schoolbooks on the sofa in the living room and joined them at the table.

Meatballs and spaghetti. I stared at the steaming red mound on my plate.

"Beverly Winslow won a dance scholarship to UCLA," said Dolores. Who cared? I poked at my spaghetti.

"The new furniture polish worked like a dream on the dining-room buffet," my mother said. Who cared?

"Joey Manila said—"

"Who cares?" I shouted, dropping my fork. "Who cares!" They all looked at me. "The Bowmans' friend, *my* friend, Jacob Mandelbaum, is dead. He killed himself because the FBI wanted him to—"

"Blue blazes, Francine!" said my father.

"Oh, honey, I'm sorry," my mother said, taking my hand. "How is Sophie doing?"

I shook my head, unable to speak for the lump the size of a Chevrolet in my throat.

"Listen to me, Frannie," my father said. "The FBI doesn't play around. This is serious. I just hope no one else winds up dead."

I studied my spaghetti for a minute. "Instead of a funeral," I said, "all his friends are going to a ball game where they'll drink beer and smoke cigars. I don't suppose I could go?" I looked at my father's face. "I didn't think so."

Sophie was back in school the next morning when Sister Basil announced, "The Los Angeles school district is considering a plan for next year to make identification tags for all students, in case of a nuclear attack and ensuing chaos."

"Like soldiers' dog tags," Sophie whispered to me over her shoulder, "to identify our dead bodies."

"All Saints will, of course, be participating in this," Sister went on. "Make sure we have your current address and telephone number as well as numbers where we might contact your parents."

"If we're dead, they'll be dead." Sophie's whispers grew louder. "In fact, all of Los Angeles will be dead. In fact—"

"Is there something you wish to say, Miss Bowman?" Sister asked.

Sophie stood up. "Instead of preparing for a nuclear attack, Sister, why don't we just ban the bomb? Then we wouldn't need—"

"Wouldn't that leave us defenseless before the Godless communists in Russia?" asked Sister. "Do you think they would apologize and destroy their weapons because an eighth-grade girl from Los Angeles asked them to? Nonsense. Russia is bent on devouring us, destroying the Church, and damning our immortal souls by—"

"Couldn't we try?" Sophie asked. "Couldn't we start here at All Saints, saying 'No killing. Ban the bomb'? And then maybe grownups would do it too. And—"

"Miss Bowman, no matter what you hear at home, you are not to bring that communist propaganda into this school. Now sit down and open your spelling book. All of you."

On the way home Sophie said, "Remember that Ban the Bomb Club I was going to start last winter? Maybe I should try again. In honor of Jacob Mandelbaum. Make signs and—"

"Oh, Sophie, you know it won't be any better this time. No one will join."

"What about you?"

I thought about my unplumbed depths. I looked down at the sidewalk. "I can't."

"Never mind, then. I can make signs by myself."

And she did. The next day when I got to school, there were hand-lettered signs taped to the walls: *Peace now! No killing! Ban the Bomb!*

Sophie was holding a large placard that read: *Sister Basil the Great unfair to students! Speak out! Defend free speech!* She carried the sign up and down the hallway until Sister appeared from our classroom, her face as red as a baked ham. Sister yanked the signs down off the walls, grabbed Sophie by the arm, and marched her into the office, Sophie waving her sign behind her back all the way.

Sophie was probably right. Without bombs, there would be less killing and less fear. And she had the right to have her opinion heard. But to my surprise I could, reluctantly, see what Sister Pete had been saying. Sophie didn't always handle things in the best way. She was stubborn, ready to argue, and certain that anyone who disagreed with her was wrong. She could drive you crazy, even if you loved her. Maybe if she changed a tiny bit, just to make her life easier . . .

After school, as Sophie and I rode home, I said to her, "You know, you really shouldn't stir up Sister so much. Call her unfair and stuff. And—"

"I know, Francine, I know. It's stupid, but I kind of enjoy giving her trouble. And I don't mind getting it back. But this is different. This matters. This is *important*. We have to make peace with communist Russia. We have to ban the bomb before we all die. And we have to stop persecuting people because of their politics, people like Mr. M." Her eyes filled with tears. "I have to stand up for what I believe, to say 'That's not right,' and put myself on the line for it. Otherwise the other side, whoever they are, wins."

What could I say to that?

We had pot roast for dinner. Dolores and I did the dishes while my mother and father listened to the radio in the living room: *The Catholic Hour with Monsignor Fulton J. Sheen,* sponsored by God.

The phone rang. "I'll get it," I said, and I did.

"Francine," Sophie said, "guess what." Her voice sounded squeaky and weird.

"What?"

"I have been kicked out of No Sinners. For good."

"Expelled? Jeepers, Sophie, how come?"

"Sister Basil the Truly Awful called my father into her office this afternoon. She told him I was disruptive, disobedient, a bad influence, and didn't belong in her school." She took a deep breath. "I guess she's given up on saving my soul. My father came home and blew his stack. I'm really in the doghouse."

"Gee, Soph, I'm sorry. Maybe you shouldn't have—"

"Spare me the lecture. I already got the big speech from my father."

"But I told you—"

"Holy Francine, who knows all and is never wrong. I

think maybe you hang around with me because it makes you look good in comparison. 'Saint Francine, whatever does she see in that nasty Bowman girl?'"

My face burned with embarrassment and anger. "What a rotten thing to say! How can you—"

"Oh, go climb a tree." She hung up with a bang.

I slammed my receiver down too. How could Sophie be so wrong, so mean, so unfair!

"Francine, come listen to this," my father called from the living room. "Monsignor Sheen is talking about young people today."

I stood in the doorway. "I know all about young people today. I am one. And it's not much fun."

"Sit," he said.

So I sat.

A teenager, said the monsignor, is like a chick just breaking the shell of the family, finding himself in a great wide world. His personality is beginning to emerge. "What do you think?" my father asked. "You feel like a chicken?"

Very funny. "Cluck, cluck," I said, folding my arms across my chest.

Teens, the monsignor said, are proud that no one understands them. They wear clothes designed to express their personalities and talk "bebop talk." "Sloppiness," he said, "is cultivated to attract attention; feelings are easily hurt. These are signs that a personality is being born into the adult world."

Did he mean Sophie had hurt my feelings as part of her personality being born? Or was it *my* personality? Or did he mean . . . Wait a minute. I hurt Sophie's feelings, too, and now that I thought about it, I felt pretty lousy. She had called to tell me her bad news, and instead of listening and sympathizing like a true friend, I had lectured her. Why, I hadn't supported her any more than Sister Pete had. Maybe I was the one who was being unfair.

My father was laughing. "What do you think, Frannie? Is he right? Are you teenagers all bebop and back talk?" Before I could answer, he waved his hand at me. "Shush. I'm trying to listen."

Monsignor Sheen then started in on "biological impulses" and "the value of purity." Holy cow, he was going to talk about sex! I would not sit and listen to anybody talk about sex with my family in the room.

I went to bed, but my mind kept spinning. Should I call Sophie and apologize? But she was the one who called *me* names. Where would she go to school now? She couldn't go back to public school. Would her father send her away to boarding school? Was I about to lose my best friend forever?

I finally fell asleep and dreamed about chickens.

31

June 1950

More Bad News

Dolores did not get a car for her birthday. She got a radio. She did not die. Sophie wasn't at school anymore and we weren't speaking. Life was boring without her.

On Saturday morning I finally finished *Mr. Roberts*. Ensign Pulver and all the men were very sad when Mr. Roberts died, and finally Ensign Pulver was more upset and angry than he was afraid. He knew that now that Mr. Roberts was gone, someone else had to stand up to the captain. Ensign Pulver remembered how Mr. Roberts had thrown the captain's palm trees overboard. The captain had gotten new trees, four of them, so Ensign Pulver went up to the boat deck and threw those trees overboard. He brushed his hands together, went to the captain, and said, "Captain, I just threw your damn palm trees over the side." I knew, and the captain knew, this wasn't just about palm trees, that Ensign Pulver was finally speaking up against what he thought was wrong.

The ending made me itchy and restless. Ensign Pulver wasn't like me anymore. He turned out to be brave.

I didn't like thinking that way, so I turned on Dolores's new radio, looking for music to distract me.

Dolores came screaming out of the bathroom, pin curls and face cream quivering. "Turn it off!" she shouted. "That's my radio and I never said you could play it. Turn it off!" I turned it off. "I may have to share a bedroom with a dishrag, but I don't have to share my radio," she said, and flounced back into the bathroom.

I had let Dolores push me around for thirteen years, and suddenly I was sick and tired of it. I took a deep breath and followed her. "You know, Dolores, you're even meaner and snottier than usual these days. I don't like sharing a room any better than—"

"It was my room first. Why did you have to go and be born anyway?"

I was mad enough to sock her, but as she turned, I could see tears making little rivers through her face cream. Attila the Hun on his mother's lap, sucking his thumb, could not have surprised me more. "Do you hate me so much," I asked her, "that it makes you *cry?*"

"Don't be stupid. I don't hate you . . . most of the time. It's just that I'm miserable. Wally and I have broken up. We're through. Finished." She sat down on the edge of the tub.

Dolores had been dumped? I couldn't believe it—not Miss Popularity. I sat down beside her. "Wally is crazy about you, Dolores. I'm sure you'll be back together in no time," I said, patting her hand.

She shook her head. "No, it's over. Wally wants to go into the Navy after graduation, and he doesn't think it's fair to tie me down while he's gone. These are my best years, you know." She stood up and looked in the mirror, smoothing her face cream and lifting her chin.

Attila the Hun was back in the fight. "I'm sorry, Dolores," I said, and I was. Now she'd be around more, and more bad tempered than ever. "I am *really* sorry."

I got up to leave and stopped in the bathroom doorway. "Now can I listen to your radio?" I asked.

"No," she said, pushing the door shut with her foot.

I lay down on my bed. I missed Sophie. Enough was enough. She and I both had been unfair, but since I was unfair first, I decided I would apologize first. Right now.

Sophie's line was busy and kept being busy, so finally I just walked over to her house.

When she opened the door, I said, right away, before she could say anything, "I'm sorry, Sophie, I'm so sorry, you were absolutely right, I was being insufferably smug and superior and—"

"Shut up, Francine," she said. "It doesn't matter. My father . . ." She began to cry.

My heart stopped. "What? What about your father?"

"He lost his job at the studio. His agent won't talk to him, and Hedda Hopper in her column said he was 'suspicious.' Oh, Francine, what is he going to do? What if he gives up like Mr. Mandelbaum did?"

I put my arms around her and squeezed. "It'll be all right. Your father will fight. He won't let those guys bully him."

She pulled away. "But how can you fight rumor and gossip and anonymous threats? How? And who? And how will we live when he can't work?" I heard voices inside her house. She wiped her eyes. "I have to go. Thanks for coming over. I'll talk to you later."

My father was mowing our lawn when I got home. He handed me a broom, and I swept up the grass clippings on the sidewalk. "It's too awful," I said to him when the *clacketa-clacketa* of the mower stopped. "Mr. Bowman has lost his job because someone said he was 'suspicious.'"

"Gee, that's tough. I doubt Bowman's a red," my father said, wiping his face on his sleeve. "Just a little pink, maybe." He put his hands on my shoulders. "Either way, this is getting more serious, Francine. I want you to stay away from the Bowmans. Do you understand me? Don't get involved."

"But what are they going to do if he can't work? They'll starve. It's so unfair! I don't think Russia should be in charge of our country or that we should let communists spy on us or anything, but it is so unfair what happened to Mr. Bowman."

My father lit a cigarette and leaned against the porch. "The government and the FBI have a job to do, trying to keep America safe and free for Americans. I don't know—maybe a little 'unfairness' is a small price to pay for security."

"But Sophie—"

"I keep telling you, you shouldn't be involved with them. We don't know what's true and what isn't, but it's serious business. Be quiet, do what you're told, and stay out of the way." The *clacketa-clacketa* began again.

I found my mother in the kitchen crushing potato chips to put on a tuna casserole. "Mr. Bowman's friend, Mr. Mandelbaum, is dead. Sophie is expelled. And now Mr. Bowman has lost his job. The whole world is falling apart," I told her.

"I'm sorry. The poor Bowmans," my mother said. "Maybe I'll make two casseroles and you can take one over there."

Knowing my mother's tuna casserole, I didn't think that would be much of a treat for the Bowmans, but it was nice of her to offer. "Dad told me to stay away from them and not get involved. That's all he ever says: Don't get involved."

"Come here a minute, Francine," she said, sitting down. I sat down next to her. "You know, your father doesn't just have one job. He has two—and the more important one, as he sees it, is keeping us safe. He thinks the best way to do that is not to get involved in anything risky." She put a handful of potato chips in front of me. "You know how much he cares about his union. He used to be quite active and go to meetings regularly. Once he even thought about running for union office. But a couple of years ago, when the union voted to go out on strike—why, he got worried that it could mean trouble for his family. So now he pays his dues and that's it. He thinks it's the best way to protect us."

She stood up and wiped her salty hands on a dish towel. "Your father and I are both a bit confused with the way things are today. So many things are better. We're at peace, there's more money, more opportunities, more optimism, but it also feels like there's more to be afraid of, for ourselves and our children. Sometimes we aren't sure what we should do. Be patient with us."

I stared at her. Who *was* this person standing there? For a minute I felt like she wasn't my mother but a stranger in glasses with her hair rolled in a sausage, a person with ideas and opinions. I thought I might like that person. "Then do you think it would be all right if Sophie and I—"

"Don't push it, Francine," she said, sliding the casserole into the oven and closing the door with a swing of her hip.

A loud wail arose from the front yard. The door slammed, little feet pounded across the floor, and Artie burst into the kitchen, his nose streaming blood.

My mother grabbed a towel and soaked it with cold water. "Sit, Artie," she said, "and hold this to your nose." Artie sat.

"We were playing a little catch," my father said, coming into the kitchen, "and the ball just tapped—"

Artie took the towel away from his tearstained face. "I don't *want* to be a man," he said. "I want to be a cowboy. Or a dog."

"Enough, Fred," my mother said. My father nodded, and that was that.

My mother made another tuna casserole for the Bowmans, and she took it over there. I was not allowed to go.

32

Flag Day

My mother had tried a new product called a home permanent, made by the Richard Hudnut Company, one of the sponsors of Walter Winchell's show. "If it's good enough for Walter," my mother had said, "it's good enough for me." Now the roll of hair at her neck was gone, and her head was a mass of tightly clenched curls.

"Mother," I said, "you look so different." I thought that I might try that myself someday. It had to be easier than the curling iron.

"It's the nineteen fifties," she said. "A whole new decade. The world is changing and we have to change with it." Now I understood the new hat and the restaurant on Mother's Day.

She straightened the seams in her stockings and twirled so the skirt of the new green-and-white dotted nylon dress swirled around. "What do you think? Wouldn't a mink stole be perfect with this?"

"Blue blazes, Lorraine," my father said, leaning back in his big chair. "Who besides the Rockefellers has a mink stole?"

"Ellie Jacobs. We play canasta on Tuesdays."

"Ye gods," he grumbled. "That could turn out to be the most expensive card game ever."

They were going to my father's boss's house for a barbecue and television. I was on my way to Mary Virginia's to help prepare our group presentation for world history: the causes and results of World War Two. I myself hoped one of the results was that the world had learned enough to prevent World War Three.

"These are for you," my mother said, handing me a box. Karl's Shoes, it said. I opened it. "Mother, red shoes!" I hugged her.

"I think you've gotten enough wear out of those old black flats," she said.

I ran into my room and changed my shoes. I stuck my feet out to admire them. They were perfect. Wait till I showed Sophie!

Sophie. I couldn't show Sophie. I was not allowed to see Sophie. I could not get involved. I looked at my feet again. Red shoes weren't as much fun without a best friend to share them with.

I sat on my bed. What was happening with Sophie? Was she going to school? Had Mr. Bowman found another job? Did they go to a ball game and smoke cigars for Mr. Mandelbaum? Were they still real sad? What was *happening?*

Dolores came into the room. She squinted at me. Her new boyfriend was picking her up, and she never wore her glasses around her boyfriends. "Is that my old skirt?" she asked. "It sure looked better on me."

Good old grouchy Dolores. It was nice to have someone to count on. "You can't see well enough to know what it looks like," I told her. "You poor dear."

"Don't be mean," Dolores said. "You should try being me sometime. Even when you're as pretty as I am, it's not always easy." Her face clouded over. "And now I have to find a new steady. Only one more year until graduation. One more year to find Mr. Right."

"Don't worry, Dolores. You'll find him and you'll get married. He'll be rich and handsome and very kind. You'll be madly in love and have three children who are so smart, they skip classes in school. You'll be president of the PTA and be friends with Bing Crosby's wife, who will invite you over to—"

"Gee, Francine, you have some weird imagination." She squinted into the mirror once more, took a deep breath, and left the room.

We all gathered in the living room. "Now listen, all of you," Dolores said, peering at each of us, "Forrest will be here any minute. Please, please, behave, so he gets a good impression of you. Francine, push your bangs out of your eyes. Father, let me straighten that tie. And Mother, could you try and look a little more . . . motherly?" She looked around the room. "Where's Arthur?"

"He's using the bathroom," my mother said.

The doorbell rang, and my father opened it. The eagerly anticipated Forrest was tall, with dark hair worn just a little bit long and deep, green eyes. He would have been a real dreamboat except for a slightly crooked nose and an Adam's apple that could put your eye out.

At the curb was parked a car. A red Ford coupe with blue fenders. A hot rod. A real hot rod. Maybe Dolores thought that car made up for the Adam's apple.

"Mother, Father, Francine, this is Forrest Fitzgerald," Dolores said.

"Call me Jet," he said, sticking his hands in his pockets. Cool. Jet was definitely cool.

"How do you do?" my mother said as Artie ran in, shouting, "Gas attack! Gas attack! Dolores went Number Two and didn't open the window!" He ran in circles around us, holding his nose, cap pistols bouncing in their fringed holsters and Rice Krispies flying everywhere.

"*Mother!*" Dolores wailed.

Forrest's Adam's apple bobbed like a cork in the ocean, and my father shouted, "Arthur Henry Green, to your room and stay there until morning. Now!"

Artie went.

"Never mind, Dolores. You and Forrest go on now," my mother said, pushing them out the front door.

"Jet," he said, his Adam's apple bobbing.

After they left, my mother turned to my father. "Fred, you can't keep Arthur in his room. It's time to leave for the Watsons'."

"I'll get him," I said.

At the door to Artie's room, I called, "Artie, come on. We're leaving." I looked around. No Artie. "Artie?"

"I'm here," said a voice from under the bed.

"What are you doing there? You'll get your clothes all dusty."

"I'm making a place for Chester to hide while I'm gone."

"Why does your bear want to hide under the bed?"

"He's afraid of commanisks and bombs." Artie crawled out. "Do you think he'll be safe under there?"

I didn't think any place was safe, but I couldn't tell Artie that. Little boys shouldn't have to be worried about communists and bombs. Neither should bears. And neither should I, but I couldn't seem to help it.

"He'll be fine," I told Artie. "Bears are tough. They can look after themselves." Unlike almost-six-year-old boys and their sisters, I thought. I brushed dust and lint off Artie's Hopalong Cassidy outfit. "Grrrr!" I shouted, grabbing for him. "I'm a tough old bear."

"Growl!" cried Artie as he ran for the door.

I called Sophie before I left, but there was no answer at her house. I never knew what a lonely sound it was, the ring, ring, ringing of a phone that isn't answered.

"I wish you were coming with us, Francine," my mother said.

"I know, but we have to get this project done. I'll be at Mary Virginia's if you want me."

"Stay away from the Bowmans," said my father. "I don't want you—"

"I know. Getting involved. Don't worry. Mary Virginia never gets involved in anything that doesn't require volleyballs and whistles."

We left the house together, my mother and father and Artie in the Buick and me heading west on Palm View Drive toward Mary Virginia's. Sophie's house was on the way, and if I happened to be passing by and I could see someone there, well, stopping and asking "How are you?" wasn't getting involved, was it?

There were no lights on at Sophie's and no car parked at the curb. The blinds were drawn, and no one had watered the roses that drooped in the yard. I sighed and walked on, resigned to an evening with Mary Virginia.

"Hurry up, Francine," she called from her front porch. "There are going to be speeches and stuff at West Los Angeles Park. And there might be boys there!"

"I don't know. I thought we were going to work on—"

"Don't be such a stick-in-the-mud. Come on. Gert and Margie are waiting for us."

We started the six-block walk to the park. "What kind of speeches and stuff?" I asked her.

"It's a celebration for Flag Day."

"Sounds boring," I said.

"Well, we're not going for the *speeches*." She rolled her skirt up shorter and pinched her cheeks.

Lots of people were gathered at the park. Some young couples had spread blankets and were eating picnic dinners. Little boys ran around shooting each other dead with sticks and twigs. A man with a tray hanging around his neck sold little American flags, and a baby slept soundly in a buggy with "God Bless America" painted on the top.

I also saw a group of gray-haired women chanting,

"Better dead than Red," and a young mother holding her baby in one arm and, in the other, a large sign reading *Down with Godless Communists!* Holy cow. Was I "getting involved" just by being here?

A black-robed bishop climbed up onto a platform, motioned the crowd to be silent, and said a prayer through a microphone. A deputy sheriff then led the crowd in singing "America the Beautiful." I missed Artie standing next to me singing, "for purple mouse's majesty," the way he always did, six-shooters swinging at his waist and Rice Krispies spilling from his pockets.

The deputy then introduced some big shot from the city council. "I'm here to talk to you today about America. And Americans," the councilman said. People cheered and waved their little flags. "Real Americans, real hardworking, God-fearing Americans, like you." He unbuttoned his suit jacket and loosened his tie. "Tell me, do *real* Americans support foreign governments?"

"No!" everyone shouted, waving their flags again.

"Do *real* Americans protect known enemies of their country?"

"No!"

Mary Virginia next to me was examining her fingernails and humming. I looked around for the Bowmans. What would they say to all this?

"Do *real* Americans think they're better than the government?" the councilman went on. "Do they question their government? Disagree with their government? Organize against their employers? Take part in strikes against their employers? Let Jews and Negroes and communists take over their country without a fight?"

The *No's* got louder and louder and came faster and faster. People didn't seem to be thinking about what the guy was saying or even listening to him anymore. They just shouted "No!" Why was everyone just yelling in agreement? Didn't anyone else try to make sense of it all?

Even if we really were in danger from a communist conspiracy, I was at that moment more afraid of the red-faced, shouting crowd than I was of communists.

Mary Virginia yanked my skirt. "There's Gert and Margie," she said.

They were carrying a flock of hand-lettered signs. "Look what we found," Gert said. "Somebody just dumped them behind the platform. Here, you can each take some." *Commies, Go Back to Russia,* one sign read. *We Hate Communists,* said another, and others screamed in red letters, *Kill a Commie for Christ.*

I put my hands behind my back. "Holy cow, Gert. Did you *read* these signs? They're hateful."

Gert looked at them. "So what?" she said. Margie and Mary Virginia shrugged.

So what? I swallowed hard. Schoolgirls in saddle shoes and pleated skirts who thought it was all right to carry signs about killing. For Christ. Didn't they understand what the signs said?

I was pretty sure Jesus never said, "Kill a commie for me." He said, "Love thy neighbor." And "Blessed are the merciful." And "Blessed are they who hunger and thirst for justice." I didn't hear anyone talking about that or carrying *those* signs around.

I should have said that to them. It was time for me to speak up. I knew it. But Gert and Margie were glaring at me. I just shook my head.

"Come on," Gert said, trying to hand me a *Go Back to Russia* sign, "let's march in front of old red Sophie's house. It'll be fun."

"Now that Sophie's gone from All Saints," Margie said, "you don't have to be friends with her anymore. Come with us."

As we stood there, a voice called out, "Hey, girls. What's up?" It was Gordon Riley from the drugstore.

Margie said "Hey" back, Gert smiled, and Mary Virginia giggled. I said nothing as I felt my face grow warm and prickly.

"Can you believe this?" he asked, shaking his head. "Loonies, all of them, the bolshevik commie pinkos *and* the crackpots with signs." Mary Virginia, Gert, and Margie dropped their signs.

"Modern thinking," he continued, "says the only way to destroy the Red Menace is through commerce. Capitalism. Good old American business know-how. Take Riley's Drugs . . ."

I stared at him in disbelief. Los Angeles was going crazy, countries threatened each other with bombs, people wanted to kill each other, and Gordon Riley thought *ice cream* would save us?

"Let's forget about all this," he said. "Come over to Riley's, girls, and I'll make you chocolate sodas. On the house."

"Oh, goodie," said Margie. "That'll be more fun than

going to the Bowmans'." She and the others walked over the fallen signs to Gordon's side.

"Are you coming?" Gordon asked me.

I *could* go with him. "My hero," I could say, grateful as always for irony. "Take me away from all this nonsense to the real world—the soda fountain at Riley's Drugs." But I didn't. Sometimes you have to forget irony and just say what you mean.

"No, thanks," I said. "I don't think I want to be friends with you. Any of you." Great. The first words I ever said to him were probably also the last. He shrugged and followed the other girls off to Riley's.

"And I'm putting these in the garbage, where they belong," I said, picking up the signs, but I don't think anybody heard me.

I put the signs in the trash can at the park entrance and left. The sounds of speeches and cheering followed me for a long way. I passed the Bowmans' house on my way home. Still no lights and no car. Still no Sophie and no Mr. Bowman.

Searchlights lit up the sky. They made me think of a prison yard or a concentration camp. I would never look at searchlights the same way again. I shivered in the warm June air.

33

A Phone Call to the Pope

A sin of omission is doing nothing when you should have done something. Mine was a sin of omission. I needed to go to confession.

As I stood in line in the dark quiet of the church the following day, I prayed, "Please, God, let it not be Chuckie."

When it was my turn, I opened the door and entered the confessional. The purple plastic kneeler squeaked as I knelt down. When the panel between me and the priest slid open, I could tell by the smell of Old Spice and cigarettes who it was. Chuckie.

"Bless me, Father, for I have sinned," I said in the usual way. "It has been one day since my last confession. . . ."

"Go on," he said. "What kind of sin could bring you back again so soon?"

"I'm not sure it was a sin, Father Chuckie."

"Just 'Father,' Francine."

"Yes, Father. I don't know if I sinned, but I saw people

doing and saying things I thought were wrong, and I didn't say anything to stop them. Being grownups, they probably wouldn't have listened to me, but I didn't even try."

"Francine, it is not up to children to teach their elders, whether they are right or wrong. Remember, 'Honor thy father and thy mother.' The child's job is not to correct but to obey, just as Catholics must obey Mother Church."

"But they were shouting hateful things and carrying hateful signs. And my friends, Father, *kids my age* think it's okay to want to kill communists. Isn't that wrong?"

"Perhaps your friends are frightened. They are afraid of communists, and instead of saying, 'I am afraid,' they say 'I hate you.' That doesn't mean they're evil. Be compassionate. Forgive them. And don't you worry so much about things. Leave it to your elders and the Church."

"But Father Chuckie—"

"That's enough, Francine. Say ten Hail Marys and a sincere Act of Contrition. You may go."

I went. I wasn't feeling particularly cleansed and comforted. You'd think that Father Chuckie, being young and modern, could have given me more help than that. *That's enough, Francine* I could get at home.

My mother and father were at the kitchen table, talking quickly in low voices.

"What's up?" I asked, sitting next to my mother.

"Luba and Nikolai Petrov have sold their store," my mother said. "They're going to live with their daughter in Mexico."

"How come? Because Mr. Petrov is so sick?"

"Someone broke into the store and poured red paint over everything. It just broke their hearts. We should go over there to see if we can help—"

"I told you, stay out of it, Lorraine," my father said.

"I know you're worried, Fred," she said, patting his hand, "but shouldn't we do *something?*"

My father looked down at the table.

I went and sat in the yard, next to the hole that probably would never be a bomb shelter. My father didn't talk about it anymore. Artie'd laid a blanket over the hole and was using it for a fort. And my mother had planted her tomatoes elsewhere.

What would the Petrovs do in Mexico? Did they have baseball there? And cherry Popsicles? My eyes stung and watered, and I didn't know if it was from sadness or smog.

That night I couldn't sleep. I kept thinking about poor Mr. and Mrs. Petrov and the thirsty roses in the Bowmans' yard. What could I do? Who could help?

Who was the most powerful man in the world? The pope, of course. I would telephone the pope. Probably they wouldn't let me talk to him, but I could leave a message with his secretary or something.

I crept downstairs, rehearsing what I wanted to say:

"Holy Father, the world seems all messed up to me. What we learn in religion class is not the way things really are. Neighbors accuse other neighbors of being communist spies. Perfectly nice people have to run away and hide because they came here from Russia. They came for freedom and they got trouble. A nice old man is dead because he wouldn't tell on his friends. My little brother is afraid of the bomb, and he isn't the only one. I am supposed to obey my elders, but they are the ones who invented the bomb in the first place. Girls in saddle shoes carry *Kill a Commie for Christ* signs. 'Thou shalt not kill,' God said, but is anyone listening? Can you maybe sort this out before we are all dead?"

Of course the Vatican phone number was not in the Los Angeles telephone book, so I called the operator.

"I'd like to be connected to Pope Pius XII in the Vatican in Rome, Italy, please," I said.

"Who is this? Some wise-guy teenager?" the operator asked me. She cracked her gum a few times. "I know you juvenile delinquents. Next you'll be calling stores and telling them if they have pop in a bottle, to please let him out. Wise guys."

She hung up.

It was a stupid idea anyway. I never would have had the nerve to call. What if the pope had answered?

34

Palm Trees Overboard

I stopped by Sophie's house on my way to school the next day. No one was there. I found a hose around back and watered the roses.

School passed in its dreary, Sophie-less way. I called her number every day but got no answer. I was surprised how much I missed her. When your thumb has a bandage on it and you can't pick up anything and nothing feels right, that's how it was with Sophie gone. Nothing felt right.

We practiced marching for graduation. There was a gap in the line where Sophie should have been, like a missing tooth in a big grin, until Sister, with a smile, rearranged us.

One afternoon I stopped by the library at lunchtime, looking for Sister Pete. "Sister," I said, "may I talk to you?"

She put down her book. "Of course you may, Francine."

"Since Sophie's father lost his job, I've been thinking a lot about communists. People keep telling me that communists in Russia and China want to use A-bombs and H-bombs to destroy us and our immortal souls. I don't know exactly what to think. Is it true that communists are evil people who want to kill us, or are they just people who believe different things? And how do we know if someone is a communist? I mean, the bad kind of communist?" I knew now how Sophie felt, bedeviled by questions that pushed and shoved to get out. "You know, people say, 'He is a communist and therefore an evil and destructive person.' Or 'He is not a communist and therefore not an evil and destructive person.'" But no one says, 'He is a communist but that doesn't mean he is an evil and destructive person.' And what if that's the truth? Oh, not awful people like Stalin in Russia, but ordinary communists. And is it right to report your neighbor for maybe being a communist if it will make him lose his job or something? And what if—"

"Whoa, Francine. Sit down." I sat. "I know we live in frightening times, with so many things to be scared of and so little certainty as to right and wrong. Monsignor Sheen says that although communism is evil, we need not fear it as much as we should fear being Godless. So I let others fight the political battles while I struggle to keep God in my heart, follow the teachings of Mother Church, and pray for the conversion of those who do not know or have forgotten God."

I leaned forward in the chair. "You mean you just ignore what is happening in the real world?"

Sister Pete smiled. "God is in the real world, Francine. I have chosen God."

"Yes, Sister." I stood up to leave, disappointed. This wasn't any help. But I sat right down again. Something else was bothering me. "Sister, I can't find Sophie and I have to see her. I feel so awfully guilty." Sister raised her eyebrows. "I let her down. When the other girls teased her in Red Rover, I didn't do anything. Or when they called her names. And the other day, when they wanted to march to her house with horrible signs, I still did nothing. Sophie will never forgive me."

"Saint Peter denied Our Lord three times and still was forgiven, Francine. I'm sure Sophie understands."

Maybe, I thought, but I wasn't sure I did. "Sophie means a lot to me, Sister. I know she acts up and doesn't always use good judgment, but she helps me think about things. She's my best friend, and I didn't do anything to defend her."

"Perhaps you will still get a chance. Just be sure that what you do is right and honest and pleasing to God."

"But how will I know that?"

"The Church gives you guidelines, Francine. And you can pray to know God's will."

Some first or second graders came in to use the library then, and our talk was over. I left feeling frustrated and confused. My questions had led not to answers but only to more questions. I wished I believed in fortunetellers. And could afford one.

When I got home, I looked through the day's mail. There was a large envelope with a Hollywood postmark. My response from Monty! Finally, after I had forgotten all about it! At last, someone with answers! I tore open the envelope.

A photo fell out, signed *Yours truly, Montgomery Clift*. That was it. No letter, no note, no word. Probably Monty had never even seen my letter, just paid someone to open his fan mail and send out photos and keep people from bothering him. *Yours truly, Montgomery Clift.*

I tore the picture into a hundred pieces. I felt like the whole world had let me down. There was no one to say, "Everything will be all right, Francine. Let's talk about it together and figure it out." I'd really thought Monty would be the one to help me. In movies the actors always knew—

And where did I think actors got the words to say? Of *course* actors didn't make up their own words. Someone— someone like Mr. Bowman—wrote the words, and actors just said them. Movie stars weren't magical beings but ordinary people like me. Only more glamorous. And richer.

I didn't want to be an actress, I realized, and pretend to be other people, and read someone else's words. I just wanted to be me, as soon as I figured out who that was.

The phone rang. It was Sophie at last. I was so relieved and excited that the words just tumbled out of me. "How are you, Soph? Where have you been? I watered your roses. Are they okay? Is your father—"

"I can't talk, Francine, but I wanted to say goodbye."

"Goodbye? *Goodbye?* Where are you? What's happening?"

"Just listen, Francine. I can't tell you anything. I'm not even supposed to be talking to you now, but I couldn't leave without saying goodbye. I mean, you were my best friend, after all."

"What do you mean 'were'? Sophie, what's going on?"

"I have to go now. Thank you for being my friend. I learned a lot from you and I'll miss you." I could hear tears in her voice. "Now I won't have anyone to tell me about movie stars and help me use my imagination and teach me to dance."

"Oh, Sophie, I've been so worried about you and missed you so much. I need to see you. Can I come over and—" I heard a click. "Sophie, wait! Sophie!" I shouted. "We'll figure something out. You can't go. I can't—" But there was only silence on the other end.

"Goodbye? . . . *Were* my best friend?" I threw down the receiver and ran out the door.

The Bowmans' car was not there, and a moving van was parked in front of the house.

The door was wide open. I went inside. It was all so familiar, all the books and pictures and the big old radio. Everything was still there, except for the photograph of Mrs. Bowman. But where were Sophie and Mr. Bowman?

"Are the Bowmans here?" I asked a beefy young mover with *Tim* embroidered on his pocket.

"Nope. Nobody's here. We just got instructions to come and pack things up and put them in storage."

"Do you know where they are?"

"Nope," Tim said.

Another mover passed by, carrying Mr. Bowman's big leather chair on his back. He shook his head. "Nope," Tim said again.

I raced from the house, my eyes streaming and my nose running. I walked and walked, crying and thinking. Where had they gone? And why? Why couldn't Sophie tell me anything?

Pictures of Sophie filled my mind as I walked: Sophie standing in the wastebasket, Sophie onstage at the speech contest, Sophie waggling the sign behind her back as she was dragged to the principal's office, Sophie smoothing her hair and tucking a lock of it behind her ear. I realized it was a soft and gentle gesture, like something a mother would do for you if you were sad or afraid. If you had a mother.

I stood on the street corner and cried. Sophie was gone. I couldn't believe it. She might still call or write me, but it wouldn't be the same as being best friends. Maybe I'd never see her again, or maybe I'd be reading a newspaper one day, and there would be a story by a crusading reporter who talked about freedom of speech and fighting for justice, and it would be Sophie. I cried even harder.

Finally I rubbed the tears off my face and started home. Was there something I could do? Some way I could fix this and bring Sophie home? But I was just one thirteen-year-old girl in Los Angeles, one scared thirteen-year-old girl. What could I do? What did it matter?

And I realized that it *did* matter. *I* mattered. I wanted it to matter that I'd been here in the world.

"Isn't it time you spoke up and took sides?" Sophie had asked me once. And now the words kept repeating in my head as I walked. Isn't it time? Isn't it time? Suddenly I couldn't stand it any longer, all the unfairness, the injustice, the fear, the bullying and the blaming. Sophie, Mr. Bowman, Artie and Chester Bear, poor Jacob Mandelbaum, the Petrovs, the droopy Patsy who would suffer all next year. I was so angry. It was wrong, all wrong!

I couldn't solve everything, but I could do something. What if I stood up to Sister Basil the Great? What if I fought this one little fight?

My footsteps slowed. Go home, I told myself. You could get into trouble. Despite the cautionary voice in my head, I turned and headed for school. I knew what I had to do.

I had no money for the bus, and it was a long walk. I heard Sister Pete saying, "Be sure what you do is right and honest and pleasing to God."

I could only do the best I could. "Dear God," I thought, "I sure hope this is okay with you."

The school looked different in the gathering darkness, creepy even, with the smoke rising from behind the building that meant Mr. Sweeney was burning trash in the big incinerator.

The lights were on in the principal's office. Sister Basil.

My stomach was all knotted up, but I forced my feet to move. I walked up to the big double doors and pushed them open, hard. They slammed back against the wall, the noise echoing in the empty hallway.

I walked quickly to Sister Basil's classroom. The familiar smell of chalk dust, pencil shavings, and old tuna sandwiches made my stomach turn. I picked up the wastebasket with sweaty hands.

I waited until Mr. Sweeney left the yard and then went out the back door. I dropped the wastebasket on the ground and jumped on it over and over, kicked it, banged it against the building again and again, until it lay crumpled and ruined on the ground. I was crying so hard that I could hardly see, but finally I got the door of the incinerator open and threw the wastebasket in. I watched the fire blaze for a minute, wiped my hands on my skirt, and turned back to the building.

I crept through the dark hall again and out the front door. I didn't know how God would feel about what I'd done, but I was satisfied. I had made a stand against Sister Basil.

I started for home, trotting at first and then slowing to a walk. No, I told myself, don't stop. Just go home. But Sister Pete's words echoed in my head: right and honest, honest, honest. "Oh crumb," I said, and turned back toward the school.

As I walked, I rehearsed. "Sister Basil the Great," I'd say, "I just threw your damn palm trees over the side." I shook my head. Sister would likely toss me out the window for saying *damn* before I really got started. I'd say it right out. "Sister, I just threw your wastebasket into the fire." I could imagine Sister's mouth dropping open and her face growing red.

What did I truly want to say to her? "Sister, it seems to me the world is full of bullies. Russia and America are bullying each other. Communists like Stalin bully people, and so does the FBI. Sophie and Mr. Bowman, Artie and Jacob Mandelbaum and the Petrovs, Betty Bailey and Patsy and all sorts of other people whose names I don't know, suffer because of bullies. I myself have been bullied into silence, but I just can't be quiet anymore. It's not right when people or groups or countries are bullies, and I think it has to stop.

I can't do anything about Russia or the FBI, but I can stand up to you. Sister Basil the Great, I think you are a bully. And I think you should stop it." That's what I would say.

My legs shook. Graduation was in five days. Would I still graduate? Would I be able to march? What would Sister do to me? She would never understand. I was pretty sure my father wouldn't, either. My mother? Maybe. I kept walking.

I hoped Sister had gone home, but the light in her office still glowed. I walked slowly into the school and down the hallway to her door. I opened the door with my sweaty hands.

Sister was writing in a notebook. I stood there watching her, my heart pounding noisily in my chest. I was Joan of Arc facing the French soldiers, Ensign Pulver confronting the captain. Oh, I knew Sister Basil wasn't evil, that she cared about us in her own way, but still, what she did and how she did it was not right. Even if Sister Basil did not change one bit, even if I got into trouble, I had to speak up.

"Sister," I said from the doorway, "Sister . . . I mean . . . I want to—"

"Francine," she said, looking up at me, "what on earth are you trying to say?"

I swallowed hard. "Well, Sister," I said, "I'll tell you."

And I did. This time I really did.

Author's Note

As the 1950s began, Americans were frightened. Communist parties had gained control in Eastern Europe, China, North Korea, and Southeast Asia. Would America be next? Were there spies and secret agents working in this country to make that happen? Who was a communist agent? How could we tell?

In the early years of the twentieth century, thousands of Americans had joined the Communist Party or other organizations later called communist or subversive. Many joined because they saw the party as a way to take a stand against the excesses of capitalism, the oppression of workers, racism, anti-immigrant feelings, and, later, the poverty and massive unemployment of the Depression. As more became known about the destructive aspects of the Soviet government, the increasingly authoritarian nature of the party, and the brutality of some of its leaders, a number of party members resigned, but in the minds of many they remained "Reds," so called because of the color of the Soviet flag.

AUTHOR'S NOTE

Some American politicians took advantage of the "Red scare" of the late 1940s–early 1950s to further their political ends. The most notorious of these was Joseph McCarthy, a Republican senator from Wisconsin from 1947 to 1957. As chairman of the Senate Permanent Subcommittee on Investigations, he claimed to be using his congressional power to uncover a communist conspiracy. In fact, although he ruined many people's lives and livelihoods by subjecting them to unfounded and unfair accusations, he never proved that one single person was a communist. The use of investigation and public accusation, innuendo, and guilt by association to discredit people came to be known as McCarthyism.

The paranoid hunt for communists and spies lasted for many years, long after Senator McCarthy was censured by the Senate and died in disgrace. More than six hundred college professors were fired because of unsubstantiated rumors about their political affiliations. Public libraries were forced to remove books by or about communists, socialists, liberals, and in some cases African Americans and Jews. It is estimated that by 1956, 13.5 million Americans had been required to pass some sort of loyalty test in order to be hired for a job.

Critics saw McCarthyism as an attack on freedom of speech and freedom of association, which they thought more dangerous than the threat of communism itself. The Constitution, they said, gave Americans the right to free speech, to join together in protest. But those who spoke out found themselves called suspicious and subversive.

Like those named "communists," they endured enormous pressure. Victims faced harassment by the FBI, loss of a job, name-calling in the press, estrangement from friends or family, physical attacks, and, many times, imprisonment. Fearful of becoming victims, Americans became increasingly conformist and conservative in manners, dress, and politics.

McCarthyism was especially harmful to writers and entertainers. In 1947 the House Un-American Activities Committee (HUAC) began an investigation into the motion picture industry. McCarthy later claimed that more than two thousand actors, writers, directors, and producers were communists, although he was never able to identify them. And in June 1950, three former FBI agents and a television producer published "Red Channels," a pamphlet listing the names of writers, directors, and performers they claimed were members of subversive organizations. A free copy was sent to everyone involved in hiring people in the entertainment industry. All the people listed in the pamphlet were blacklisted—denied employment—unless they proved they had "reformed," which meant naming other supposed "communists."

Many of those accused could no longer find work. Some had their passports taken away. Others were jailed for refusing to give the names of people who might be communists. Ultimately over three hundred twenty Hollywood actors, screenwriters, and technicians were blacklisted. At least two of them committed suicide, and three others died as a direct result of their harassment. Jacob Mandelbaum is a fictional victim of the anticommunist "witch hunt" and a symbol of those who lost their livelihoods or their lives because of McCarthyism.

At the end of 1949 the Soviet Union announced the successful testing of an atomic bomb. The fact that their communist enemy now possessed a nuclear weapon, followed by the invasion of South Korea by communist North Korea in June 1950, left the American people even more frightened and began an era of fear and covert warfare that became known as the Cold War. A Gallup poll taken in 1950 found that 70 percent of the American people believed the Soviet Union wanted to take over the world, 75 percent thought American cities would be bombed in the next war, and 19 percent thought the next war would wipe out the human race.

The newly formed Federal Civil Defense Administration (FCDA) and the Atomic Energy Commission (AEC) acted to calm the fears of the public and disseminate information on how to prepare for and survive the expected nuclear attack. Both agencies published materials to educate the public, in which the catastrophic results of a nuclear attack—such as burns, radiation sickness, and death—were played down.

"Surviving Under Atomic Attack," from the FCDA, sold for ten cents and began with this cheerful statement: "You can live through an atom bomb raid and you won't have to have a Geiger counter, protective clothing, or special training in order to do it." Nonetheless, sales of Geiger counters and so-called "radiation-proof" suits soared.

The FCDA also distributed information on building your

own bomb or fallout shelter or preparing your basement to serve as a shelter. There were serious debates over whether people had the right to shoot outsiders who tried to get into their shelters.

Air-raid sirens were set up across the country and tested monthly. Cities made plans for the evacuation of their residents, based on the assumption that there would be some minutes of warning before an attack. Air-raid drills were held regularly in thousands of American cities.

Schoolchildren were taught to "duck and cover." I was one of them. At a shout of "Drop!" from the teacher, we crawled under our desks and covered our heads with our hands. This sounds ridiculous today, given what we now know about the destructive power of nuclear weapons, but at the time we did what we were told and hoped for the best. Walking home from school, I used to scan the skies in fear, cringing at the sound of airplanes and looking for a handy ditch to jump into in case of an attack.

Catholic schools in the 1950s, when I attended, practiced more humiliation and corporal punishment than they do now. I didn't know any nuns who made students stand in a wastebasket, but I attended schools where nuns beat boys' hands with a ruler, where girls and boys were punished by being made to change into each other's clothes, where faces with a hint of makeup were scrubbed with Ajax cleanser. I knew students who were told that their divorced parents were going to Hell. My school had nuns who spent their days red faced with anger, but there was also a sweet young novice with red hair peeping from beneath her veil who was warm and kind, and there were dedicated nuns who sacrificed their time and themselves for "their" girls. Not all nuns were, or are, Sister Basils.

There actually was a baseball team named the Hollywood Stars, and they did wear shorts for a few games. And by the way, Jacob Mandelbaum was right. In 1950 Frankie Kelleher of the Hollywood Stars led the Pacific Coast League with 40 home runs. Such a slugger, that boy, as Jacob would say.

If you wish to know more about the early 1950s, here are some places to start:

Michael Barson. *Better Dead Than Red! A Nostalgic Look at the Golden Years of Russiaphobia, Red-Baiting, and Other Commie Madness.*

Sally Belfrage. *Un-American Activities: A Memoir of the Fifties.*

JoAnn Brown. "'A Is for Atom, B Is for Bomb': Civil Defense in American Public Education," *The Journal of American History,* June 1988.

Civil Defense Office. National Security Resources Board Document 130, "Survival Under Atomic Attack." At www.schouwer-online.de.

Dan Epstein. *20th Century Pop Culture.*

Eric F. Goldman. *The Crucial Decade—and After: America, 1945–1960.*

Lois G. Gordon. *The Columbia Chronicles of American Life, 1910–1992.*

Joy Hakim. *A History of Us: All the People,* Book 10.

Stuart A. Kallen. *A Cultural History of the United States Through the Decades.*

Milton Meltzer. *Witches and Witch-Hunts: A History of Persecution.*

Howard Zinn. *Postwar America: 1945–1971.*

KAREN CUSHMAN was born in Chicago and moved to California with her family when she was ten. She now lives on Vashon Island, west of Seattle, with her husband, Philip.

Ms. Cushman is the author of the Newbery Medal book *The Midwife's Apprentice*, the Newbery Honor book *Catherine, Called Birdy*, and *Matilda Bone*, all set in medieval England. Francine Green is the third Cushman protagonist whose story is set in the USA, joining Rodzina ("prickly but endearing" —*School Library Journal*, starred; "a delightful, thoroughly Polish heroine"—*The New York Times* Book Review) and Lucy Whipple ("an irresistible teenager"—*Kirkus Reviews*, pointer).